FACELESS

KATHRYN LASKY

HARPER

An Imprint of HarperCollinsPublishers

Library of Congress Cataloging-in-Publication Data

Names: Lasky, Kathryn, author.
Title: Faceless / Kathryn Lasky.
Description: First edition. | New York, NY : Harper, an imprint of HarperCollins
  Publishers, [2021] | Audience: Ages 8–12. | Audience: Grades 4–6. | Summary:
  Growing up in 1943 war-torn England, thirteen-year-old Alice and her older sister
  Louise are members of a centuries-old spy clan, but when Louise decides to spy for
  the enemy, their bond is changed forever.
Identifiers: LCCN 2020052741 | ISBN 9780062693310 (hardcover)
Subjects: CYAC: Spies—Fiction. | World War, 1939-1945—Fiction. | Sisters—
  Fiction. | Secret societies—Fiction.
Classification: LCC PZ7.L3274 Fac 2021 | DDC [Fic]—dc23
LC record available at https://lccn.loc.gov/2020052741

Typography by Joel Tippie
21 22 23 24 25 GV 10 9 8 7 6 5 4 3 2 1

First Edition

For evil to flourish, it only requires
good men to do nothing.
—*often attributed to Simon Wiesenthal*

CONTENTS

Within five years I, with his majesty's blessing, had created a new secret agency, the most adept in the world of intelligence and counterintelligence. Thus far the Rasas, as in "tabula rasa" in reference to their completely forgettable, nearly blank faces, have endured. We of course refer to the agency now only as the Company. God willing and the empire be blessed, we shall endure for centuries to come. Our greatest triumph was a few day ago, July 29, 1588. The defeat of the Spanish Armada!

—from the 1588 diary of William Morfitt, spymaster to King Henry VIII

Mid-January 1944

LONDON, ENGLAND

ONE

THE UNVEILING

"How are we this morning, Louise?" It seemed odd that the doctor should be speaking to this great lumpy head swaddled in bandages.

"Good, I think." The three disembodied words flowed out of the dark hole. Alice felt a peculiar queasiness wash through her at the sound of her sister's voice. She regretted now that she and her mother had gone to the British Museum yesterday. There had been a mummy there, wrapped in burlap. Tufts of ginger hair sprang from the top of its head, escaping the cloth. And now she felt as though she was standing at the bedside of another mummy. Her sister, Louise Eleanor Winfield.

Her mother, Posie Winfield, held Alice's hand in a hot, sweaty grip. Alice wondered if she was thinking of that same

3

mummy from the museum—what had it been called, Clarissa? Yes, Clarissa. How stupid. How British! If the mummy was Egyptian royalty, why would the archaeologists use such typically English names? But they did—Clarissa, Peregrine, Derek. All cozy in galleries sixty-two to sixty-three.

"Louise, sweetie, it's me, Mum. And Alice."

"I'm not blind." Louise lifted her hand from the bedcovers and pointed toward the two eye slits in the bandages. Her hand was a welcome sight. It looked the same.

"How are you feeling?" Alice asked.

"Excited."

"As well you should be!" the doctor said buoyantly. "The unveiling is always an exciting moment. Or moments, I should say, as we do take our time. Never rush," the doctor added softly. "Now Sister Agatha will help me snip the bandages." As Sister Agatha entered, it was as if an immense seagull had flown into the room. Nurses at St. Albans belonged to a Catholic order that shunned ordinary nurses' caps for voluminous wimples, cloth headdresses last in fashion during the Great War of 1914–1918.

"You'll see some stitches, of course," Dr. Harding continued. "But not as many as you would have, say, a year or two ago. We are now using a new dissolvable thread for a lot of the sutures."

What Alice saw first was not stitches but bruising. Splotches of metallic gray tinged with rose. Her sister looked tarnished like old silver. It wasn't the shock she had expected,

4

but there was something, despite the bruising and the swelling, that was essentially different about Louisa's face. Alice couldn't help but wonder if she would ever do this herself. Would this be like a kind of divorce from one's self? Would you have to get to know yourself all over again?

"Excellent!" Dr. Harding's voice cooed like a dove as he admired his handiwork. "Very little swelling considering this stage of the game." Alice saw her mother wince at the word "game."

Game. That's all it is for him—a game!

Alice thought back to the conversation they had had in the doctor's office less than half an hour before. The preparation conference, he called it, four days following the surgery. This way they might all be ready at the unveiling.

Her mother had popped up from her chair the moment Dr. Harding entered the room. "Everything all right, doctor?" She was a veteran agent for the Rasa division, called the Company, under the authority of MI6 , Britain's Secret Intelligence Service. But of course the Winfield family was not "undercover" with Dr. Harding. He was one of perhaps four or five plastic surgeons who worked on these special agents when they decided they no longer wanted to serve. And that was what Alice's sister Louise had decided. She no longer wanted to be part of the most elusive and secret of all the branches of the British intelligence agencies.

But why? Alice had asked herself this a dozen times every day since Louise had announced this decision. Louise was six years older than Alice, and she was celebrated as much as a spy could be. Two years ago, Louise had been advanced to level A missions. Her work had been impeccable. Her renown was not public, of course, but her reward had been increasingly sophisticated missions. Why would she give all that up?

The Winfield family was part of an ancient tradition dating back to the court of Henry VIII and William Morfitt, the spymaster for the king. It was Morfitt who had, over a short stretch of time, come in contact with two people whose faces were completely forgettable. Nonfaces that were like tabulae rasas, or blank slates. These void-like faces haunted him. They were not officially spies when he first encountered them. Indeed, many of these people were petty criminals. But what perfect spies they would make, he thought. No one would ever remember them. The king agreed. And thus the division later called Rasas was formed.

The Winfields came from a long line of Rasas. The Rasas had served kings, queens, and country for hundreds of years, through countless wars. And now Alice's big sister was leaving. She and Louise had done so many missions together. Not level A for Alice yet, just B and C levels. But Louise had promised to be her guide. Now she felt abandoned. And yes, shocked. Not by this new tarnished face that Louise had been given, but because of the promise she had broken.

"Everything is perfect," Dr. Harding was saying. *No, not everything!* thought Alice. "I'm sure you'll be pleased with the results, and more importantly, I think Louise will be too.

She's been very clear in what she wanted all along. Definitely not film-star looks, like Greer Garson or Vivien Leigh. Ever since the movie *Gone with the Wind*, everybody is going for the Vivien look—the delicate little nose. But no film stars for our Louise . . ." Alice winced as he called her "our" Louise and waved his hand dismissively. In one simple gesture, he was banishing some of the most beautiful and talented women in the world.

"My ideal patient. Together Louise and I worked to create something highly original." That was the first time the queasiness had seeped into Alice's stomach.

The doctor had cracked a rather toothy smile. It seemed to Alice that he had about five too many teeth crammed into his mouth. He continued, "I've never enjoyed being a copyist." He paused briefly. "Now before we go in for the unveiling, let me show you something."

He rose from his desk and, reaching for a cord, pulled down a diagram of a human face, its features and the underlying musculature. "This"—he gestured at the diagram—"helps me explain the procedure that I performed on Louise and other cases like this." By "cases," he meant other Rasa agents who wanted to leave the service and acquire a unique and memorable face.

He then pointed to a poster on the wall with twelve digits, 1.61803398875. "Do you know the significance of that series of numbers?" he asked. Alice and her mother shook their heads. "It's a ratio." He paused briefly. "A very particular ratio that's known as the Golden Mean."

There was a dim flickering in Alice's head. Geometry with Mr. Leighton. "Something with architecture?"

"You're on the right track, Alice. The Golden Mean comes to us through Greek philosophy. It is the ideal ratio between two quantities. It suggests an organic wholeness. Even our bodies and our faces follow this mathematical ratio. But no humans' faces adhere to this ratio as unswervingly as you members of the Rasas. But this does not mean that you are all identical, or 'clones' of each other. Look at yourselves, Mrs. Winfield and Alice. You are not clones. You, for example, Mrs. Winfield, have auburn hair, while Alice has . . . has . . . a rich brown." *Liar!* Alice thought. Her hair was mousy brown.

The doctor continued. "Your brow, Mrs. Winfield, is a bit broader than your daughter's, and your eyes perfectly placed in relation to your brow and your nose. Just as Alice's are for her narrower brow. Everything balanced perfectly.

"However, if you translate these ideal relationships and shapes into a human face, the result is pleasing rather than memorable. Human faces become memorable when they deviate in some slight way from the norm, from the Golden Mean. The slightly crooked nose. The lips that have a certain unevenness between the top and bottom. The eyes that droop ever so slightly and give a dreamy effect to a gaze. And then of course there are those people who are afflicted with micronathism—in varying degrees."

8

At this point her mother, Posie, blanched. "Micro what?" Alice could feel her mother's growing discomfort as the doctor continued.

"Chinlessness—a condition in which the lower jaw recedes a bit too much and is smaller than the rest of the face. There was a de' Medici with this condition. It might have been the old gent himself, Cosimo." Alice could feel her mother becoming increasingly nervous. She knew her parents had known other Rasas who had undergone surgery, but maybe her mother was also thinking of this as a sort of divorce, and rejection by her own daughter. Although when Louise had first announced her intentions, Posie had said, "If this is truly what you want, dear, of course."

But at this moment, when the doctor uttered the word "chinless," Posie Winfield, known as the most unflappable of agents for her complete composure in the most dangerous of circumstances, now seemed to crack.

"Doctor, what have you done to my daughter?"

"Nothing she didn't want, dear lady." He leaned across and patted her hand. *Paternalistic bastard,* thought Alice. He had just laid out a virtual buffet of facial deformities, and he expected her mother to remain calm. "All I have done with Louise's face was to create a slight, barely perceptible deviation from the Golden Mean."

Alice watched as her mother's eyes brimmed with tears. Her mouth seemed to move silently around the words "barely perceptible."

Alice reached out and grasped her mother's hand. "Let's go see her, Mummy."

At the sound of the word "Mummy," Posie snapped back. Cool as the proverbial cucumber. Composed. Imperturbable Posie Winfield now seemed to grow an inch. The Rasas did have an innate ability to assume a variety of postures, to acquire, almost instantaneously, subtle qualities that were quite transformative when needed. They could be veritable human chameleons. Posie turned to her daughter. "I'm sure it will be all right."

"All right" was such a weak expression, Alice thought.

Now, twenty minutes later, they stood before Louise as Dr. Harding snipped at the bandages to unveil her. And Louise was different, so different.

"The swelling will go down substantially over the next day or two," the doctor said. Those words seemed to unleash within him a deluge of clichés. Louise would be "right as rain . . . good as new . . ." The bruising would recede, and she would not look tarnished, but "penny bright."

But, thought Alice. *How will I ever deal with this change in my own sister?* Her older sister, who Alice had known for all of her thirteen years. For some reason, this reminded Alice of when she was four years old and had lost her Fuff—a pink bunny that she slept with every night. Louise had generously given her her own stuffed animal, Puppa the puppy, to comfort her. Ultimately, the bunny was mercifully found again, and Alice finally outgrew it when she went to summer camp in Scotland with other Rasa children.

But would she outgrow her sister, now that she looked so different and was no longer working for the Rasa network? It had taken her so long to catch up with her, or so it seemed. *But no,* she scolded herself. She'd be the same old Lou Lou, inside. *I'm being childish,* Alice told herself. She reached for Louise's hand and gave it a light squeeze. Yes, they were six years apart, as Louise was nineteen. But suddenly those six years seemed as vast as the Atlantic Ocean.

"Lou Lou, it's me, Alice," she whispered.

"I know, silly. I told you, I can see!"

TWO

"THE TRUE ME"

Alice remembered that day when Louise had told her that she was going to do it. They had been sitting in a café in Grantchester, a small village near Cambridge, where they had been living for just a few months. It was two days after New Year's. Their father was still on a mission in Berlin. He had been there now for a year and a half, and they were in the fourth year of this dreaded war. Louise had called it her New Year's present to herself—"A New face for the New Year," she had exclaimed at midnight when the clock struck the chimes in the village and 1943 slid into 1944.

"So, you're going to do it, Lou Lou, really and truly what you said last night?" Alice had asked.

"Yes!" Louise snapped. "Look at that waitress over there." She nodded in the direction of a door that led into the kitchen. "Don't be obvious. But she's staring at us. She can't remember our names or quite who we are. We've been in here . . . what, maybe fifteen times? But she just can't place us. I'm sick of it. I'm sick of the missions, sick of . . ." Her shoulders slumped. "Of . . . of being so . . . so forgettable. I've grown tired of it. I was always frustrated by living this lie. I'm ready to leave. Mum says it's fine."

"I . . . I won't forget you. Not ever."

"Of course you won't, and I won't forget you. We're Rasas, but first of all, we're family."

Somehow Alice did not find this all that comforting.

Lily the waitress made her way across the room with their tea and what passed for buttered toast these days. No butter, and there was only the grayish duration bread, due to the rationing of flour. On the tray was a thimble-sized pot of honey.

Alice saw her pause briefly and then peer at them harder. Louise was right. Poor thing was trying to remember them—almost desperately. To Lily it must be as if their faces were ephemeral—like liquid reflections in a pond. It was as if the still water was suddenly ruffled by a slight breeze, and any wisp of memory was now dissolving beyond the waitress's grasp, making Alice and Louise completely unmemorable. Alice tried her best but still couldn't understand why this would drive Louise to have the surgery.

Lily set the tray down.

She nodded at Louise. "Sorry, dear, about the honey. They

just cut our rations." Dear was always a safe name for a girl one couldn't quite remember.

There was no one else in the café, and when the waitress retreated to the kitchen, Alice leaned across the table toward Louise.

"So what did the surgeon say when you saw him?"

"He said it's a relatively simple operation. The recovery time is brief. The swelling usually goes down within three to four weeks."

"And the Company pays for all this?"

"Yes, that's the deal. I believe MI6 shares the cost."

"I wonder why? Seems sort of extravagant. I mean, it's wartime. Even honey is rationed now, and this . . ." Alice made a low, throaty sound of disgust as she looked at the gray bread. Toasting it did nothing to improve the color. "But you're really sick of it? The missions and all? You did so well. You got to do A levels before almost anyone else even close to your age."

"I know. I was not much older than you are now when I was first sent to Norway—mopping floors in you-know-where just after the Nazis invaded." She paused. Then, under her breath, she muttered, "Fertilizer plant indeed!" Then giggled.

Mopping and mapping had been Louise's assignment. She had been part of an early spy operation. The mission was to map the Norwegian hydrogen production plant called Vemork, and observe the guard schedules. The Norwegians

14

themselves thought they were producing fertilizer, but espionage work in Germany revealed that this was heavy water, as it was called. The factory could produce not only fertilizer, but also the key to an atomic weapons program that the Nazis were developing.

"Well, it's gone now! And you certainly had something to do with it." Alice's eyes were bright with admiration.

There had been two previous attacks on the plant that had failed. But then almost a year ago, in February of 1943, there was success and the plant was destroyed. Norwegian saboteurs, using maps created by Louise during her undercover work in Norway, had skied across the pine forest of Telemark wearing winter whites and, like ghostly apparitions, descended on the plant. Their backpacks were filled with explosives and fuses. They had trained in Scotland, perfect preparation for the grueling expedition that would require these spies to scale icy mountains in pitch-darkness, ford rivers, and ski across treacherous terrain.

Alice reached across the table and grasped her sister's hand. "Louise, you're a hero."

"Definitely an unsung one." She laughed.

"I would sing to you loudly!" Alice said in a hushed voice. "Don't you feel proud of how you helped in . . . in . . ." She dared not mention the actual name of the plant or the expedition, which had been called Operation Gunnerside.

"Yes, of course. But you know so much of what we do is boring. Stultifyingly boring."

"Like mopping floors. But you said the skiing was fun. And there was that handsome fellow. Anders."

"Oh yes, Anders!" Like fleeting clouds, a dreamy look passed across Louise's eyes. "But did he ever remember me? Hardly!"

"But you said there was that one time he kissed you."

"*Almost* kissed me that one time, and then I was extracted from the mission right after. He missed so many opportunities before that, as it took him the longest time to remember me enough to even want to kiss me." Louise sighed. "I knew it wasn't my cup of tea. Anyone can leave the Company. You think they want soft agents? Unhappy, whiny ones?"

"You never whined. I'm the whiner in the family, if anybody is."

"No, you're not. I just did my job, and I knew when I didn't want to do it anymore."

"But what will you do now?"

Louise looked about. There was no one sitting close by.

"Bletchley," she whispered. "I scored quite high on the exam."

"You did?"

Louise nodded. "I just have to be patient and wait."

Alice thought a moment.

"I know you went to classes at Cambridge."

"Believe me, if we get through this war, women will be allowed to enroll officially at Cambridge University. Some of the best code breakers are women who sat in the back rows of the lecture halls."

The Winfields had moved close to Cambridge, England, directly from Scotland, where Louise had been part of the training program for the forces responsible for blowing up the plant. The move was somewhat of a reward for services rendered by their family. Their father had delivered some superb intelligence while in Berlin. For almost three years, Alan Winfield had been stationed as an operative in Germany, and he was responsible for the early data and information concerning the heavy water.

He worked as a chauffeur for the government—or what in Germany was called the Reich. Reich was the German word for "realm" or "regime." Realm was a much prettier-sounding word. It conjured up thrones and queens and kings in crowns and beautiful robes. But Reich was so harsh sounding. Blades, clanking armor, and annihilating obedience. And yes, that little guy with the ugly toothbrush mustache and the dark madness in his eyes. Adolf Hitler.

The Reich Research Council was the government center for atomic physicists. Her father had chauffeured them all, the top physicists of the Reich: Otto Scherzer, Abraham Esau, Erich Schumann. But it was Werner Heisenberg who chatted the most, and from whose careless lips he had first heard the words "heavy water" and "Vemork."

Louise had always dreamed of attending a great university. So as a reward for her services in Norway, in the late autumn of the previous year, 1943, Posie, Alice, and Louise were moved to a new home within two miles of Cambridge University. Louise's entrance for lectures was of course arranged by the Company. Alice, in the meantime, had entered the local school. No posh school for her. Not the local pricey preparatory school, whose students carried crimson-and-orange school satchels. Her school colors were tan and black. And no special book bags were issued, although there was talk of changing the colors, as they had become favorite colors for many Nazi military divisions.

Alice's main challenge in the local school was not to appear too advanced. For she was extremely intelligent, as all Rasa children were. The Rasa had a facility for picking up languages, especially, and every summer they were sent to language camp. It was not unusual for a youngster to have mastered five or six different languages and dialects by the time he or she was sixteen. It was called language camp, but they learned many other things there as well. It was where they took their first parachute jumps and began flight training.

Alice had made no close friends in Grantchester, for even in a small village school it took forever for her classmates to remember who she was. But this was as it was supposed to be. They were supposed to blend in unremarkably, seamlessly. Anonymity was their business—their family business. It never really bothered Alice that much. She had her sister. She had her mum—and soon, if things worked out, she and her mother might be reunited with their father. Louise would not join them now.

But Louise as a code breaker? She'd never have imagined her sister sitting around with a lot of Cambridge mathematicians. Though the code breakers at Bletchley were at the very epicenter of intelligence, monitoring the secret communications of the German forces.

Bletchley, an ornate mansion set in the middle of a beautiful park, was a closely guarded secret. It housed the code and cipher school for the British government. At Bletchley, they were devising a machine to decipher Nazi code, specifically working to crack the German Enigma code. They produced ultra intelligence, according to MI6 and the Company.

The more Alice thought about it, the more she realized that Bletchley was a logical place for an ex-Company person to go. Especially one with a new face. Now those young men Louise had sat next to in the lecture halls would surely remember her. Alice had always heard Louise say, "It takes the fun out of flirting if you know the fellow won't remember you the next day."

Alice sighed. "It's sort of exciting, I suppose. . . ." Alice's voice dwindled. Then she became suddenly animated. "So, what do you want to look like?"

"Me! I want to look like *me*."

Alice giggled. "But that's impossible. I mean, don't you want to look like, say . . ."

"Greta Garbo?" Louise said with a trace of contempt.

19

"Why not? She's not exactly hideous, you know."

"Nor is Joan Crawford, or Hedy Lamarr or Lana Turner." All the movie stars they saw at the cinema were gorgeous in their own ways. And memorable. "I want to be me. Just me." She sighed. "You know, Alice, the other night I went to that pub with Lucy. And this fella is sitting near me and asks if he can buy me a pint. Here's exactly what he said. 'Did anyone ever tell you that you look like Rita Hayworth?'"

"The movie star?" Alice asked.

"Indeed! The movie she's starring in, *Only Angels Have Wings*, was playing at the cinema right across the street. He had just seen it."

"What did you say?"

"'I'm not Rita Hayworth. No red hair, and I wear mine up in a French twist.'

"'Doesn't matter,' he answers. 'You remind me of her. I see a red glow in your hair, and if you let it down, it would tumble just like hers.'" Louise took a sip of her tea, then gave a harsh laugh. "Alice, that movie is in black and white!"

"Doesn't seem to matter." Alice began to giggle.

"What are you laughing at?"

"Did I tell you what happened when I went to the apothecary the other day to pick up that medicine for Mum?"

"No. What happened?" Louise leaned in closer.

"Mr. Jenkins, he screws up his eyes and starts studying me. Then finally he says, 'Blimey, I can't ever remember your first name, dear. Is it Minnie?'"

"Oh no!" Louise gasped.

"Yes! He'd most likely been to the cinema and seen that cartoon. Minnie Mouse. It's playing there now."

Louise sighed again. "Did I also tell you about Mrs. Black-more?"

"The lady down the lane from us?"

"Yes. She comes running up to me on that little road off Cromwell Square. I had some parsnips and things in my shopping bag, and she stops short and says, 'You're Jillian, aren't you?' And I say, 'Jillian? Who's Jillian?' And she says, 'The butcher's daughter. I heard a rumor that he has some pork chops in.'"

"I get it, classic WTS," Alice said.

"Exactly. Wishful thinking syndrome. She'd probably been yearning for them. She just wished me into the role of Jillian Wirth, the butcher's daughter."

"I know Jillian from school. She's not exactly a beauty. Terrible spots and rather unfortunate hair. Thin and limp."

"But you remember her, don't you?" She leaned back in her chair. "Case made!" she announced with a trifle of smugness. Then her tone quickly changed. The satisfaction evaporated.

"No one can really know us. Such is our fate, Alice." Her voice was mournful. "But it doesn't have to be."

Alice thought for several seconds. "But what will you be after your surgery? What will the real you look like?"

"I don't know, but I can't wait to see me! I know that 'me'

is there. Inside me someplace. I want to be me." She paused. "The true me!" she whispered, as if this was a deep secret. "And Dr. Harding, the plastic surgeon, is supposed to be a real genius."

At that moment Lily the waitress returned. "Anything more, ladies?"

"No, that will be all, thank you," Alice replied, smiling up at her.

Lily seemed to beam. "Did anyone ever tell you that you look a lot like Shirley Temple?" Alice resisted rolling her eyes. Her hair was straight as a stick, unlike the child movie star's.

"No curls."

"But I can almost see them! I'm not kidding. You're the spitting image. You should go to the cinema. *The Blue Bird* is playing around the corner now, and Shirley stars in it."

"Okay, maybe."

"Bye-bye, Shirley!" Lily called out as the two sisters left the café.

THREE

SWAPPING VOWELS

"It will settle," Dr. Harding had said in the hospital room at the unveiling. It was as if he had been speaking of a house settling on its foundations. Or perhaps, Alice imagined, the ground after an earthquake. The features of Louise's face were almost the same, but ever so slightly different . . . just rearranged, perhaps? *Not the right word*, Alice thought as they sat down at the dinner table. Louise's nose was still in the middle, and her mouth was where it should be. "Disturbed" was a better word than "rearranged." Disturbed, but not in a bad way, yet an interesting way. The swelling had almost vanished, as had the bruises. She no longer looked tarnished.

Posie set down the casserole in the middle of the table. "Tomorrow night, I promise, no more snoek. We'll use the last coupon in my ration book." It was the fourth time that

23

week they had eaten tinned snoek, a South African fish that had escaped being rationed. Alice looked across the table at her sister and wrinkled her nose. Louise attempted a nose wrinkle herself but failed. Her nose was still slightly swollen but nice. Alice hadn't dared ask Louise if this face across from her was the one her sister had sought. She recalled her sister's words from that day in the café: *I want to be me. The true me!*

In a sense, Louise Winfield, or Lou Lou, still looked basically the same. But there was something definitely more memorable about her face. It was as if it had been quickened in some way that would make it not so forgettable. Nevertheless, Alice would sometimes hear their mum give a little yelp if she came around a corner in their house and Louise was coming the other way. It was not as if she was encountering a complete stranger, but still someone she hadn't expected to see.

It was the next evening, the evening of no snoek casserole—as Alice came to think of it—but instead stuffed peppers, when Louise made her big announcement. "Lou Lou, pass the white sauce," Alice had said.

"Please pass the white sauce," her mother corrected.

"Lou Lou, please pass the white sauce," Alice repeated. Louise giggled a bit. A little private giggle, as Alice would come to think of it. Perhaps a coded communication with her newly released inner self.

"Another minor correction," Louise said softly, and slid her eyes first toward their mother and then Alice. "From now

24

on, please don't call me Lou Lou. Dispense with the nickname, kindly." Although there was nothing kindly in her voice. It was brittle.

"Of course, Louise," Alice murmured. She felt as if something had collapsed inside her.

"Ah!" Louise exclaimed. Both Alice and her mother, glanced at each other, confused.

"Ah, what?" Alice asked.

"*Louisa*, not just Louise."

"Why?" Alice asked.

"It's just . . ."

"Just what?" Alice pressed. She felt irritation rising in her. Something was happening to her sister, and it had nothing to do with her face. What *had* that doctor done to her? The irritation began to quickly subside into fear. *Why am I afraid?* she wondered.

"It's just more . . . well, I just think it's more elegant. More memorable. Goes with my face better."

"Really?" Alice asked in a shaky voice. How could swapping one letter, one vowel for another, really do all that? Then the irritation returned. "Perhaps I should change mine to Alicia, even though I haven't had plastic surgery? There could very well be a tiny Alicia scampering about inside of me. Just gasping for air. Dying to be released." Alice's voice had bloomed into full, scalding contempt.

But Posie, always attempting to broker peace between her two strong-minded daughters, began to chatter away. "Of course, dear. I had thought of naming you Louisa, but your

25

father felt it seemed heavy freight for a delicate little girl. You were so delicate."

"Louisa" laughed. "I suppose Papa would call that 'schwere fracht' now," she said.

Alice and her mum exchanged horrified glances at Louise's admission of her father's location. Louisa appeared engulfed in a tidal wave of sudden remorse.

"I'm sorry! Sorry, sorry!" She jumped up from the table and rushed over to kiss her mother. Posie looked at her daughter with a steely glare.

"Sorry, won't do. You said it, Louise! Out loud!"

"I said it softly, Mum. No one could hear. The cottage isn't wired."

Posie pushed her plate away. "I'm not really hungry. I think I'll set the kettle on for tea."

The incident, though not forgotten, was never again mentioned. Everyone kept calm and carried on, as the motivational posters instructed; they had been plastered up all over England.

Louisa's face continued to heal. The puffiness, within another two weeks, was completely gone. Her complexion was no longer tarnished, and she was back to the proverbial English rose. Alice was just returning home from an errand when she saw a small cluster of girls who often walked the two miles to and from Cambridge University for lectures. They stopped at a window of the millinery shop to admire a copy of the queen's hat.

"It's just perfect for wartime, I think," one girl was saying.

"Yes, you're right, Florrie," Louisa replied. "You don't want anything too cheery and colorful. No dyed ostrich plumage. Just nice tawny pheasant feathers. Not Buckingham Palace tea-party fashion." She sighed wistfully. "Those days are behind us."

Alice thought that Louise had seen her, for she had looked directly toward her at some point in this short exchange. Alice briefly hesitated but then decided to interrupt. "Uh . . . but they are primary feathers, wing feathers for flight, Louisa."

Louise turned now and looked at her straight on. Looked at her and through her. There wasn't a flicker of recognition for at least five seconds. In Alice's school experience, it would take her teachers, and those who would eventually become her friends, at least a month to remember who she was. She had so often seen this same gradual glimmer of dawning recognition during that first month—the blankness as they raked their memory to figure out who this face belonged to. Where had they seen it before? Then the dim flickering melted at last into a gleam of recognition.

"Oh, Alice!" Louisa laughed awkwardly. "Forgive me," she said, turning to the other two girls. "Florrie, Jean—this is my sister, Alice."

For a moment Alice actually felt unsteady on her feet. It was as if she had been snagged by a strange kind of riptide, pulled away from her own sister, who stood on the beach, watching her but not knowing her. But now Louisa bid her friends goodbye and then, tucking Alice's arm snugly beneath hers, they walked off in best-of-friends fashion. But the problem was that Alice and Louisa were not the best of friends. They were sisters. And that was different. Completely different.

"Oh, Louisa!" Florrie called out. "When can you come over and teach us to dance the Charleston?"

Louisa laughed. "Maybe tomorrow"

"Terrif! You know, Alice, nobody can dance the Charleston like your sister!"

Alice smiled. "I know, she is really good!"

Alice was haunted by this encounter. She dared not mention it to her mother. For she also noticed that Louise was beginning to spend a lot of time in front of the two mirrors in their cottage. Alice observed as Louise regarded herself in the mirror, tipping her head as she practiced a variety of smiles that showed the dimple Dr. Harding had created. The scent of a perfume that Louise had begun to wear wafted down the hall. Since she was no longer a spy, Louise could indulge in perfume now too. She had bought it as soon as she came home from her surgery.

"Is it working?" Alice asked as she watched her dab on some perfume.

Louise gave a small yelp. Again there was the blankness in her sister's eyes, this time followed by a flash of absolute terror. *She actually thinks I'm a thief, a home invader!* Then Louise shook her head as if to clear it.

"Oh, Alice. It's only you! You sneaked up on me."

"Crikey, Louisa! You left the door open. I wasn't sneaking

up on you . . . Lou Lou in the loo!"

"Thanks!" Louisa snarled. And began to shut the door. But Alice put out her foot to stop it.

"What are you doing? I want some privacy."

"Just one question before you slam me out."

"You're being dramatic."

"Am I now? Oh, that's rich." Alice could not hold back. "I think you're the dramatic one. You look like an actress trying out expressions for an audition."

"I'm not an actress, and I'm not auditioning for anything except Bletchley. It's rather nerve-racking."

"Well, I was wondering: is the dimple working?"

"What are you talking about?" Alice could almost hear Louisa's teeth grinding.

"You've told me that it takes the fun out of flirting if you know the fellow won't remember you the next day. So how are the fellows in front of the lecture hall now? Calling up for dates?" Alice couldn't stop herself. She knew she was being spiteful, but she couldn't help it. She felt as if a river of bitterness was flowing through her.

There was an earsplitting sound as Louisa slammed the door.

And the mirror cracked.

Alice ran downstairs to the parlor where her mum was knitting. She didn't want to alarm her mother, but she had to say something.

"Mum," she gasped.

"What was that sound I heard upstairs?"

"Oh . . . uh . . . the door was left open in the lavatory and the wind . . . came through the window and slammed it. I'm afraid the mirror is probably cracked . . . a bit." Yes, blame it on the wind and not on her sister's vanity.

"Oh, I can take it to the glazier. He might be able to patch it up." Her mother sighed. "I know Louise—I mean Louisa—spends quite a bit of time in there. Dr. Harding gave her all sorts of ointments to put on."

Not just the ointments, Alice thought. She suddenly had an image of Narcissus from the myth, kneeling as he peered at the liquid-silver pond and began to fall in love with his own reflection. The myth came back to her vividly. Transfixed by his own image, Narcissus stared at his reflection until he disappeared, and all that was left was a flower—a daffodil. But it was the opposite with Louisa. She was not disappearing. Alice and her mum were. Just two days ago there had been another little yelp when Louise-*ah* entered the parlor and said, "Oh, Mum, you surprised me."

"Me? What's so surprising?" Posie had said. "Don't I sit here every afternoon, knitting for those dear soldiers? Working on a batch of amputation covers now. Cozies, they call them, like tea cozies." She harrumphed. "But there's nothing cozy about having your hand blown off. I'll tell you that!"

Alice remembered this moment distinctly, for there had been a strange yellowish light in the sky and they could hear the distant rumble of air raids. Alice recalled thinking that at that moment, another young man's limbs were being flung into the bloody coffers of war.

She continued to look at her mother now.

"Louisa was at the mirror again."

"Well, I can get it fixed, and there's always the mirror down here in the hall."

Don't encourage her, Alice wanted to say.

Why was her mother so dismissive? She felt a sudden compulsion to talk to her mother about this, to ask if she had also noticed a deeper change in Louisa.

"Mother?"

"Something else, Alice darling?" *Darling*—the word struck Alice. Her mother hadn't called her that since they had lived on Eaton Square in London. She must be daydreaming now of those days when they had lived in a very fancy house with an entire staff of servants. She had often called Alice and Louise "darling" then. It was part of their cover. Fancy titled people used different words. What was "dearie" now, or "dear," would have been "darling" in their Eaton Square days.

Posie had assumed that aristocratic posture, and her voice had instantly acquired the porcelain timbre of an upper-class British lady, the wife of a duke or a lord. She could have been sitting in the royal box at Ascot, discussing the king's newest thoroughbreds. Of course, the Ascot races had not been run since the beginning of the war. But Alice knew that her mother often slipped into these dreams. Perhaps because of the many past roles she had played as a spy. She was fine now with this new role, Posie Winfield, purely lower middle-class.

This was her legend, as it was called in espionage. The

legend was the term for a spy's background, supported by documents, along with a vast number of memorized details. According to Posie Winfield's new legend since she had arrived in Grantchester, she had once served as head house-keeper in one of the grand houses in Hampshire, where her husband had been a chauffeur. She was very proud of her eldest daughter, the first Winfield ever to attend university. High hopes for the younger one. Content to knit for the wounded soldiers and live on a smallish stipend in this mod-est, slightly dilapidated cottage.

Praying and knitting, that's what she did now. Oh yes, and her work with the ladies of St. Mark's Church. Father Morris had finally remembered her name and put it with her face. Well, not really her face. But a face suggested by a dream he had one night about his sister, who had died some years before. The sister was named Phyllis. In his mind, it wasn't such a leap from Phyllis to Posie. Now he often commented on Posie's resemblance to his late sister. But none of this bothered Posie Winfield. She was used to it. For Posie was a spy among spies, and one of the best, the shrewdest. Had she not been a spy, she could have been an actress. She could play any role.

"Uh . . ." Alice was hesitant to interrupt her mother's day-dream.

"Out with it." Posie sighed, gazing out the window. "Though we're still in February, it does seem that the days are actually quite a bit longer. Spring is what—another three weeks away? A blessing. More light to knit by for the poor lads. And less darkness for the Nazis to bomb us."

"Mum, do you think Louisa has changed?"

"Changed? Well, of course she's changed. My goodness, when I read about how those plastic surgeons work. You know they actually lift the whole face off at one point during the surgery. That's why they call it a face-lift. But all the scars are hidden. Not a stitch to be seen unless you look behind the ears. They have the cleverest ways of disguising their stitchery."

"But I mean in other ways—not just her face. She said she wanted her true self to come out. 'The true me,' she called it."

"Hah!" Posie laughed. "Makes it sound like one of those Russian dolls where one fits inside the other . . . now what do they call them? Matryoshka dolls!"

"But Mum—whoever this inside, innermost doll is, she's not like Lou Lou."

"Nonsense, dear." She paused. "Louisa." Her mother enunciated the word with particular care, giving the final vowel a flourish. "She's still the same old Louise, or Lou Lou. Remember, beauty is only skin-deep."

That might be true, thought Alice, but there was something else inside this new Louisa. It was beginning to feel as though her true identity was a maze that Alice had become lost in.

Posie gave a groan and got out of her chair. "Come along now. Help me pull down the blackout curtains. Soon enough it will be as dark as Satan's heart."

Half an hour later, Alice and her mother had been seated at the dinner table for four or five minutes.

"Where's Louisa?" her mother asked.

"Primping, undoubtedly."

"Now, Alice, don't be jealous."

"Mum! I am not jealous of my sister and her utterly artificial face."

"Well, then don't be nasty. Give her a bit of a break."

Break. Just like the broken mirror that got sick and tired of her reflection! Alice thought.

"Your sister is still there beneath her new face. You haven't lost her, Alice."

"But Mum, in a funny way I feel I have."

"No, you haven't. I promise you." Then she tipped her head back.

"LOUISA!" Posie screeched loudly. "Supper!" Posie winked at her daughter, and Alice giggled.

She was using her Lina the fishmonger voice. Posie had once served as a spy during the First World War, the Great War, in a fish market in Belgium, stuffing coded messages into the gullets of cod and bream.

"Sorry, sorry." Louisa swirled into the room. She flashed her mum and sister a smile that really set off her dimple. Soon it was replaced by a grimace.

"Snoek again!"

"I know, it's hard to flirt with a snoek," Alice murmured.

* * *

They had just taken the first bites of the dismal fish casserole when they heard the creak of a wagon on their lane.

"Jeremy!" Posie Winfield exclaimed in a hot whisper. Alice's eyes opened wide with excitement. Louisa's would have too, but they were still a bit swollen. Posie was at the front door before the knock came. She opened the door and gave a little gasp. Jeremy Walpole stood with a bottle of milk. "Nearly shortchanged you on your order today." Outside was the milk float, now a horse-drawn wagon because of gasoline rationing. His horse stomped the ground. "Oh, thank you, Jeremy! Thank you so much!"

"God bless, Mrs. Winfield."

The girls and their mum all rushed with the bottle of milk to the kitchen sink. They poured out the milk, which would be unusable, as it was not milk at all—just some white liquid. Then they fished out an oiled piece of paper hidden inside it. Posie held it under the tap and turned on the water. This was a twist on the invisible milk ink commonly used in cryptology. That was strictly elementary stuff for schoolkids, Alice thought.

She could not tear her eyes from the paper. This could be it. Her first A-level mission. The message was beginning to appear under the running water, in an acid-based ink known as blue tone. It had been invented by the newly formed SOE—Special Operations Executive. This combined the secret agencies concerned with espionage, sabotage, and reconnaissance into one force. Within seconds, the message would dissolve without a trace.

"'Silly times are here again.'" Posie read it in a whisper and looked up at her daughters.

"We're in business again, girls!"

"Not me," Louisa said softly. Was there regret in her sister's voice? If there was, it was too late, as there was no turning back. Suddenly Alice felt a terrible sadness wash through her.

"It's okay." She reached out and squeezed her sister's shoulder.

"Oh, don't worry." Louisa grinned. The dimple flashed, but her eyes seemed dead. Not a gleam of light. Not joy, not sorrow, not regret. Nothing.

"True. Not you, dear." Posie reached out and touched her daughter's new face.

"But I'll do my bit, Mum." Alice smiled. Louisa only gave a sort of half smile. An enigmatic smile at best. The smile of a stranger, Alice thought. *Or perhaps a kind of ghost.*

"I know you will, dearie."

Alice watched as her mother tipped her head and studied Louisa's face. Was her mum really sensing something different? It seemed to Alice that Posie Winfield was searching for her daughter, thinking that Louise had to be in there someplace. Yes, someplace in there was the child she had known and given birth to, loved and still loved. "I'm sure the job at Bletchley will come through for you, dear."

March 1944

BERLIN, GERMANY

FOUR

"WILLKOMMEN IN DEUTSCHLAND"

The shadow of a man in a trench coat and fedora hat stretched across the airfield on the Scilly Isle of Gugh, which dangled off the main isle of St. Agnes like the stubby tail of a dog. The hat cast an angled shadow over the man's face. His thick glasses had misted in the fog, erasing any light emanating from his eyes. He was calm, yet radiated an inescapable intensity in the white murk of the night.

This was T. The director of the Company. He handed an envelope to Posie Winfield and another one to Alice. They had both changed into their flight suits. Then, in a somewhat raspy voice, he began to speak. "Level A." Something ignited deep inside Alice. She glanced at her mother, whose mouth was now slightly open in anticipation. The hat was angled over the man's face. His eyes were now just a blur behind the

39

thick lenses. A fleeting trace of a smile could be detected.

"Yes, Frau Schnaubel!" Her mother's cheek seemed to twitch as he uttered the name. "May I call you Lotte? And your daughter Ute." Alice grasped her mother's hand. It had been almost three years since her father, Alan Winfield, had gone to Germany. And a year since he had been promoted from his job as chauffeur for Reich Research Council and inserted as the top mechanic. He was now the Direktor des Fahrzeugbetriebs, director of motor vehicle operations, in the Bendlerstrasse garage of the war department. And they were to be reunited at last!

T began speaking softly. "Here are your passports and the other documents. Don't open them until you reach two thousand feet. Read them and follow protocol." Then another figure strode across the runway, where the aircraft stood waiting.

"Ah, your chariot awaits you. And its driver, RAF pilot Stefan Bacik." He gestured to the approaching figure. "The fog should be clearing soon enough for takeoff."

"Guten Abend, Frau Schnaubel and Fräulein Schnaubel. Yes, the fog is clearing, but it might chase us across the Channel." He smiled at them. These were the greenest eyes Alice had ever seen. He held his helmet under one arm, and his blondish hair flopped over his forehead. Charming. It was the only word Alice could think of for the way it fell across his brow.

Although he had an almost unidentifiable accent, she knew from his surname that he was Polish. Part of the Royal

Air Force, and a unit known as the Kosciuszko squadron, or the 303. The 303 was renowned. Fleeing Poland, these airmen had made their way to England through Rumania and France. Their contribution was indispensable in the Battle of Britain. They were considered superior to British pilots because they had learned to fly in primitive, outdated aircraft and were unaccustomed to the sophisticated equipment of the British planes. Therefore they could fly through any conditions—who needed radar?

There were no formal goodbyes or expressions of good luck. Alice and her mother followed the pilot quickly to the aircraft. The canopy was slid back. There was a short ladder attached to the port side, where one could enter both the front and rear cockpit. Stefan climbed in first, and then Alice and Posie squashed themselves into the rear cockpit.

"Lucky you're both so fit." Stefan laughed as they strapped on their helmets and parachutes. Then added, "You know the drill."

"Ja, ja," Posie answered. "Mir sind scho mol gsprunga." We've jumped before.

Her Swabian accent was perfect. She sounded exactly like she had been born and raised in that region in the southwestern part of Germany, where the accent was quite distinct from that of Berlin. Alice had done perhaps twenty or more jumps when she was in Rasa camp, but this would be her first actual mission jump.

From the rear cockpit, Alice and Posie watched the

altimeter on the instrument panel. It didn't take long to get to two thousand feet. They both opened the packets that T had given them.

Inside were their German passports and their legends, with all vital information.

Alice looked at her passport picture. *The Golden Mean, that ideal mathematical ratio between two quantities,* she thought as she studied it. *A face no one would ever remember, including Stefan.* Alice sighed. He had seemed to have a smile just for her when he commented on how she and her mother were fit. But she knew that within minutes her face would soon become just a blur, tucked away in the back of his mind, irretrievable.

Alice, however, set her gaze on his helmeted head and retrieved every detail of his face. She recalled his eyes—so green. What exactly made his face so memorable? His nose was quite thin and sharp. Toward the tip it bent down ever so slightly. There was something lovely about his mouth. When he smiled, there was an unevenness to his lips that made the smile rather appealing.

Alice hadn't done much kissing in her life, but she could imagine. Unfortunately, the last person who had kissed her, back when she was thirteen, thought she looked like Princess Margaret. She supposed she should have been complimented, as Princess Margaret was considered quite pretty . . . but she often looked stuck-up in her photos.

Stefan's hair was actually a blondish red. And so was the

stubble on his cheeks. It was obvious that he had not shaved for a day or two. But it was those green eyes that got her! In the rearview mirror they appeared to look back at her now. Crinkles emanated from the corners and sloped down to join lines that were too old for such a young face. They added an indefinable quality. What was it? Empathy? Einfühlung. Yes! That was the German word. So much better than the English one. He smiled now and gave her a wink. She felt herself blushing fiercely and began to read the documents in the envelope by the light of her pocket flashlight.

The first was the passport.

> *Cover name: Ute Maria Schnaubel*
> *Code name: Sunflower*
> *Case officer code name: Wotan*
> *Date of birth: May 15, 1931*
> *Place of birth: Tuttingen, Germany*
> *Profession: student*

"Aah," she murmured. Of course, Tuttingen was in the heart of Swabia. She should have known. Schnaubel was just about as Swabian as one could get.

Field Marshal Rommel himself was Swabian. Known as the Desert Fox, he was commander of the German and Italian forces in the North African campaign. So she would have to speak with a Swabian accent. No problem. She had picked it up within a week at language camp two years before. The first thing she had learned was the inescapable *sh* sound. "Fährsht du heut' mit däm Bus?" Are you taking the bus today? The German for "bus" rhymed with "puss," not "fuss."

Alice and her mother unfolded the single sheets. They were sticky to the touch.

The message was brief.

You are now officially part of Operation Valkyrie. OV is a plan first devised by the German Reserve Army to support Hitler, in case there was a general breakdown in civil order as a result of the possible Allied bombing of Berlin or an uprising of the millions of foreign forced laborers.

Your mother [unnamed] will work in the office of the General Army Office, which is part of the OKW, Oberkommando der Wehrmacht. She will work for the reserve army, the very center of Operation Valkyrie. You [unnamed] will attend the Hermann von Haupt Gymnasium, one of the elite secondary schools in Berlin. Your admission has been arranged. You shall be enrolled for the spring term, which began the first week in March. If you perform with consistent excellence, you will become eligible for a part-time position after school in the New Reich Chancellery, the headquarters of the Greater German Reich. Your complete legend will be given to you upon reaching your destination and shall be written in CODE ONE.

I have a a complete legend! Alice thought. This was a mark of achievement. She wasn't just being tacked on to her mother's legend as an offspring. She had, of course, played very minor roles in other operations that her parents had gone on. But she had never been so significant that she warranted a legend of her own. She read the last sentence of the message.

> *On conclusion of reading this, follow standard protocol.*

Alice glanced at her mother, who had begun nibbling at the sweet paper. She had to eat it slowly, as it tended to upset her stomach. Not Alice's. Alice loved the stuff. It tasted just like the jelly candy that she had spent her pocket money on when she was little. She began biting the paper. She hardly had to chew it, as it dissolved almost immediately.

Alice continued, studying the back of Stefan's head as he guided the plane. Finally she looked out the window. They were coming down through a cloud layer into what seemed to be shifting densities of darkness. Soon the night would be stripped away and the land below would reveal itself. No lights, of course, were visible.

The intercom crackled. "We are approaching the drop zone, ladies."

They had descended to eight hundred feet. Stefan cut back

on the speed. Posie would be the first out. She slid back the canopy of the rear cockpit and began to climb out and down the rungs of the ladder on the port side. Then she arched her back into the wind. This was the ideal exit posture. She would be in a freefall for close to sixty seconds before her chute opened.

Within seconds Alice followed, pushing her hips forward to achieve that perfect curve her mother had mastered after so many jumps. Her chin up. Her face tipped toward the sky. Then there was that indescribable feeling of the freefall. There would be total peace as the air cushioned her, as she tumbled through divine nothingness, but ever so softly. *This is freedom, this bliss. The world is my friend. The air loves me. I am one with all.*

She emitted a small gasp as she saw Stefan raise his hand and wave. He smiled broadly. Even with his helmet and goggles, she could see the lines radiating out from his eyes. *And I am just wind, blurred and forgotten,* she thought.

But it was a lovely night. She felt her parachute open. The stars spangled the sky. It was perfect. She loved the blackness of the night that provided a foil for any light. Without the darkness, the light would become cheap and tawdry. A candle's flame less worthy. A hearth no longer cozy. Inscribing the darkness were those spring constellations—Leo, the Lion, embraced by the Crab and the Maiden, Cancer and Virgo with its bright blue star, Spica. They were all there, blazing like ornaments as the earth leaned toward the sun.

She pulled her feet and knees together. She needed to be slightly curled before landing and ready to buckle her midsection so that her feet would absorb the impact.

She touched ground, then immediately threw herself sideways to distribute the landing shock along the five key points of her body—balls of feet, side of calf, side of thigh, side of hip, and side of back. *There!*

It was a perfect landing. She heard running footsteps approaching as her parachute still billowed.

"Willkommen in Deutschland, Fräulein Schnaubel."

FIVE

TOGETHER AGAIN

"Wieder zusammen, meine Lieben, Lotte und Ute." Alice watched as her father, Alan Winfield, better known in the city of Berlin as Gunther Schnaubel, raised his glass of schnapps. Welcome, my dear ones, Lotte and Ute.

His eyes glistened with tears. It did not matter that he welcomed them in their new language, and now called them by these new German names. They were used to such things. When Alice had been small, they were in Russia, in a tiny village in the Crimea on the beautful Sea of Azov. She had been called Anoushka, which meant "grace" in Russian. Her father was Mikal, her mother Elizaveta, and Louise had been Maria. And in Finland, just before the war broke out, her father had been Aapo, her mother Basak, Louise was Kaipo, and Alice was Gaia. It didn't matter what language they spoke. They knew who they were, even though their names might sound strange to their ears.

She remembered the Shakespeare play *Romeo and Juliet*. They had seen it just four months before, when they had traveled to London. She thought of Juliet's speech bemoaning the curse of her last name.

> *'Tis but thy name that is my enemy:*
> *Thou art thyself, though not a Montague.*
> *What's Montague? It is nor hand, nor foot,*
> *Nor arm, nor face, nor any other part*
> *Belonging to a man. O, be some other name.*
> *What's in a name? That which we call a rose*
> *By any other name would smell as sweet;*
> *So Romeo would, were he not Romeo call'd . . .*

Alice had written a school paper on the passage and received an A-plus from Miss Evans. Miss Evans, who could never quite remember who Alice was if they met in the village. "Oh yes!" she had exclaimed the first time. "No, no, of course you're Alice, Alice Winfield. But truly, I think of you as Juliet now. That paper was excelllent." At least half a dozen times more, Miss Evans had called her Juliet.

Her father looked up from his Kasspatzel. The smell of the dish was divine. All Alice could think was, *It's not snoek!* No more fish casserole, thank god. No, this was a Swabian specialty of dumplings smothered in cheese and topped with carmelized onions, all baked together. Spaetzle was popular throughout Germany, but she knew that what made it a Swabian specialty was the carmelized onions. She had learned this from Rasa summer camp, when she'd taken the advanced program in regional German cooking and lifestyle.

"It's clean here." Her father cast his eyes around the cozy dining room. By clean he did not mean tidy. He meant that their apartment above the Bendlerstrasse garage was not wired. No bugs recording them. Then he added, in a lower voice, looking down as if talking to the dumplings, "Aber man kann nie vorsichtig genug sein. Das Zimmer ist sauber." One can never be too careful. The room is clean.

"I'll get the strudel." Her mother started to get up.

"Nein . . . nein, Lotte. I'll get it. You've been traveling. You must be tired."

Two minutes later, he came back with an apple strudel. But again it was Swabian style, with lingonberries mixed in with the apples. He set the pastry in the middle of the table. "Courtesy of Frau Meister, who will be working with you at OKW, in the general army office of the chancellery."

Alice took a bite of the strudel. It was heavenly. The lingonberries added a slight tang. She close her eyes and savored the taste. She heard the fire crackling in the little porcelein stove that warmed the room. It was all becoming slightly surreal.

She wondered where the pilot, Stefan, was now. After they'd said goodbye, the plane had dissolved into the fog that had chased them up the Channel, then across the northern tip of the Netherlands and all the way to a potato field on the east side of the Elbe River. And now, after a two-and-a-half-hour ride, they were here in Berlin.

As delicious as the strudel was, Alice felt herself nodding off. "To bed, leiben. The necessitites for the rest of your legend are in your bedroom. You have three days to study them before you start school." Her father paused. "And oh, by the way. There is a gramophone in your room, so you may listen to music. And a set of headphones. Just turn it on when you get into bed."

"Of course, Papa." (No more Dad or Father.) "And what shall I be listening to?"

"Richard Wagner's operas. The Ring cycle."

"Oh yes, I remember we heard it in camp, two summers ago."

"Hitler's favorite operas, you know." He paused. "Those Valkyries!"

Of course, thought Alice. *The Valkyries, the choosers of the slain*. In the Norse myth that had inspired the opera, the Valkyries were the winged young women who swooped down over the battlefield and picked up the heroic soldiers who had died. They flew them to Vahalla, the majestic hall, the warriors' paradise.

But there was more to her father's offhand remark than met the eye. She felt a shadow of apprehension. Something more would be coming. But she knew she must wait. Be patient. Although this was her first A-level mission, she was aware that there was a pace to these things. For a mission to be flawlessly executed, timing was everything. So in the meantime, she would listen to the music of Wagner's greatest operas and work to find clues within them.

Rasas could absorb information in a number of different ways. And music was one of the most pleasant ones. These were fantastical operas filled with giants, beautiful maidens, gods and goddesses, and all varieties of mythical creatures.

Alice loved her bedroom. It was tiny, like a ship's cabin. The efficiency of the small space was extraordinary. Her bed could fold into the wall. In a wall adjacent to the bed was a fold-out desk. A stack of papers had been set up on top. These were "soft necessities." Once she had mastered the material, most of it would be burned—not eaten like the sweet paper. She would certainly have had a stomachache from consuming all that, for the stack was at least three inches high.

She got undressed. Turned on the gramophone and began to listen to the opening chords of the first scene of *Das Rheingold*. The oboes were beautiful, and then the French horns came in. The music coursed through her like the mists of the river where the three beautiful Rhine maidens guarded the treasure—the golden ring.

SIX

In addition to German opera, there would also be popular culture to absorb—including comics. She had read some of these comics already in other countries, and they were truly funny. She particularly loved the Max and Moritz, which were almost like comic strips. She had first encountered the comics about two naughty boys at her Rasa camp— untranslated. It was an easy way to learn some German. Max and his good friend Moritz were two very clever boys who committed all sorts of devilish tricks that ranged from the very violent—like putting gunpowder in the schoolmaster's pipe—to the more harmless high jinks of putting beetles in their uncle's bed.

The next morning, Alice found a letter addressed to her, slipped under her bedroom door by her mother, presumably;

attached to it was a pamplet with a picture of a German girl with blond braids standing on a moutainside. Her arm was raised in the Nazi salute. At the top of the page was a dark eagle, the symbol of the Nazi party. She began reading the neatly typed note clipped to the cover.

"Welcome, Ute, to Jungmädelbund Group 22 of Berlin, District 5 of the League of German Girls for those ten to fourteen. You have already been certified to be of racial and ethnic German heritage—Aryan, with no contamination of foreign blood, and free of hereditary diseases. We understand from your record in Swabia that you have reached the highest levels that can be attained for girls of your age. You are nonetheless required to register at the League of German Girls administrative offices.

"However, despite these qualifications being met, you must now attend preparatory exercises in order to become a full member of Group 22 in your present home in Berlin. These consist of participation in a Jungmädelbund meeting, a sports afternoon to include a test of your courage known as the challenge, and a lecture about the tasks of the Jungmädel."

This was not news to Alice. She had heard all about the Jungmädelbund since before the war broke out. They were like a diabolical version of the Girl Scouts in America or the Girl Guides in England, which Alice and Louise had been part of. Alice had started in the youngest Girl Guide group as a Rainbow guide, and then advanced to a Brownie pack.

This year she would have become a full-fledged guide. Louise had been a Ranger but had become bored with it two years before her mission in Norway.

Alice glanced toward the desk. A new item had been added to the pile of soft necessities. Neatly folded on top of the stack of papers was some clothing. She went over and peered down at a crisp white shirt and a black kerchief with a brown leather knot. She knew she would not be able to wear the neckerchief until she had passed the Jungmädel challenge. Alice heard the door open and saw her mother. "I guess I have to do the challenge again."

"Yes, the Swabian girls' league is apparently not as stringent as the Berlin one." Her mother gave her a wink. They both knew that Alice had never taken the Swabian challenge to begin with. All part of the ruse. "You want some toasted mutter brot and hot chocolate?"

"May I eat it here at my desk?"

"Of course." Her mother smiled. There was work for her daughter to do.

With the extraordinary concentration with which most Rasa children were endowed, Alice had to master the nearly one thousand acronyms for all the miltary departments and the street maps of Berlin, as well as more mundane details about the Hermann von Haupt Gymnasium, where she would go to school.

By the time Posie Winfield returned with the small tray of hot chocolate and bread, she could tell from her daughter's posture that she was in a state of dluth, an old Rasa word indicating deep concentration. It was a derivative of the Scottish Gaelic word "dlùth aire." Each Rasa reached this state in a different way. Posie herself would count her pulse rate in her wrist. Alice would tip her head and blink for five seconds very rapidly, until it was as if she could see the most basic elements of the information in front of her eyes, of what she was studying—every detail and dot and how they were connected for meaning. At that point every single one of her millions of brain cells was ready to receive enormous amounts of information.

As Alice mastered each batch of information, she would come out from her bedroom and slip reams of papers into the lovely porcelain stove. When she went back into her bedroom, her mother would close the flue of the stove after six minutes or so, and scoop out the ashes. She would rake through them to make sure that there was not one scintilla of the written words left. She had to be sure they were clean ashes.

Near noon, Alice brought out another batch of papers.

Posie looked up from her knitting. "Your last batch?"

"Almost."

"Good. Colonel von Stauffenberg is coming for tea soon." She carefully observed Alice's reaction.

"Aaah yes!" she said with definite enthusiasm. Alice saw her mother give a quick smile. Stauffenberg was possibly a fios. MI6 might call such a person an asset, but that didn't encompass the full extent of this spy's capabilities. And that was what the elegant Count Claus Schenk von Stauffenberg was—an incredible asset to British intelligence.

The count was a lieutenant colonel in the German army who had served in both Russia and Africa. A year before Alice and her mother arrived in Berlin, he had been gravely wounded in Tunisia when his vehicle was hit by Allied fighter bombers. He had lost his left eye, his right hand, and two fingers on his left hand.

And though a hero, he had become a traitor—not to his country, but to Hitler. He had joined a secret resistance movement. That part of the pages that Alice had read was decidedly short on details. Apparently his cover was so deep and the plot so dangerous that Alice trembled as she read the document. And now she was about to meet him! But she would not know for a while if he was her fios. Such things were not immediately revealed. Soon she would learn where the signal sites would be, for her to leave chalk marks. The marks, uninterpretable to anyone else, would signal her contacts where to go for a coded message, or where to make a brush contact, as it was called in the spy world, where the message or an item could be exchanged. She must always carry with her a piece of chalk. A mark on a predesignated place in the city, a mailbox near a subway station, a specific lamppost with such a mark—this would be the signal that she needed to contact an agent.

She was a bit nervous. How did one shake hands with a

man who only had one hand with three fingers remaining? And would he wear an eye patch, or have one of those eerie glass eyes? Eye injuries had been especially common during World War I. There were several Rasa who had lost an eye. They would immediately retire, for along with their lost eyes they lost their spy cover—facelessness. Such faces were forever memorable now.

Three hours later, Alice heard the clock toll on the southwest corner of Bendlerstrasse and the Bendler Bridge. In her dluth state, Alice had memorized a detailed map of Berlin. Less than a quarter mile from their garage in the Bendler block, there was a clock that tolled the hour. Three o'clock, time for tea. And with the sound of the chimes, she heard a knock on the door of their apartment. Stauffenberg, the Gentleman Warrior, as her father called him, had arrived.

Alice got up, straightened her skirt, and rushed to the mirror, where she quickly rebraided her hair. This detail of braiding her hair had been emphasized in her reading. There was a peculiar statistic listed, that eight out of ten girls between the ages of ten and fourteen wore their hair in braids. Most often just two braids, but occasionally as many as eight braids were worn. With more than two, the braids were wrapped around the head in a style called the Gretchen. But she didn't have enough hair for eight braids, nor enough time.

She leaned toward the mirror and pinched her cheeks for a little color, then put on her dirndl apron and went to the parlor.

"Herr Colonel Stauffenberg," she said in a whispery voice. He immediately smiled, a broad and beautiful smile. He clasped her hand in a strong grip, between the stump of his wrist on his right hand and the three remaining fingers on his left. She was surprised by the strength. Her first thought was of the warmth that emanated from that beautiful face. He wore a patch over his missing eye, but the other was deep blue. He had dark hair, high elegant cheekbones, and a straight nose.

In Germany's eyes, he was not simply a hero, but an idol. Idols are idolized for their remarkable beauty or the mesmerizing spell they can cast on people. But true heroes, Alice thought, were models for bravery and decency. The man who stood before her was simply a decent man. So what she was seeing was the handsome exterior that encased something even more dazzling inside. The Gentleman Warrior in front of her was definitely an enigma, as much as the Enigma code they were trying to decipher at Bletchley, where her sister wanted to work.

"Kleines Fräulein Schnaubel, it is so nice to meet you. Just thought I'd stop in for a chat with your mother while your father works on my automobile. Fuel injector problem."

"Oooh!" Alice opened her eyes wide.

"You know about fuel injector issues?"

"Yes, a series 89654800?" Alice replied.

"My goodness!" the count replied, clearly impressed.

"She is the daughter of a mechanic, Herr Colonel, and has a gift for mechanical things." Posie Winfield offered.

"Well, I'm sure you will do very well at your school, Hermann von Haupt. Although I'm not sure if they teach the young ladies auto mechanics." He chuckled.

SEVEN

THE HIGHER DAUGHTERS

"Heil Hitler!" Alice jumped to her feet, along with the nineteen other girls in her classroom, as she raised her arm in a slant. This was only her third period at the Hermann von Haupt school, but each time classes changed and a new teacher entered, this was the practice. The teacher would then reply, "For the Führer, a triple victory."

Alice slid her gaze toward Birgit, her guide sister. "Which class is this?"

"Racial awareness. Or RA, we call it," Birgit whispered as the teacher, Frau Mueller, pulled down a canvas from a map rod. It showed a black-and-white photograph of two dozen or more people. She then turned to the class.

"I understand that we have a new student among us today." She took a small piece of paper from her pocket. "Fräulein

Ute Schnaubel. Welcome, and please come forward."

Alice stood up and walked to the front.

"Ute, can you tell us a little bit about yourself?"

"I . . . I come from Swabia, a small village near Augsburg."

"It might be small, but I hear that you achieved the highest level in your Jungmädel group."

"Yes, that is true, but I must now be tested here. . . ."

Frau Mueller whisked the air in a gesture of dismissal. "I know . . . I know. I think it is silly. It is as if they are saying that because you are from a small village, somehow this doesn't count. But it does. You are a big strong Aryan girl, and now we shall prove this."

From a desk drawer she took a set of calipers, an L-shaped metal device with two hinged legs that was used for measuring the circumference of one's head or the length of one's nose.

"What if she has a Jewish nose?" someone giggled.

"Hardly," Birgit hissed.

"No talking, girls!" Frau Mueller said sternly. "We don't make jokes about Jews. We just try to restrain or deport them."

"Along with others," someone added.

"Of course," Frau Mueller said, and then broke into a huge smile. "Well, my goodness, Fräulein Ute Schnaubel has the measurements of an angel. I have never seen such perfection."

"Thank you," Alice murmured. She supposed she should

indicate joy or relief or some positive emotion, but she only felt a bit nauseous. This kind of "education" was too much to stomach.

And for the first time since she had arrived in Germany, she wondered about her sister, Louise. How was she doing in England without them? A message had come through to Posie on a brush contact the day before, that Louise had indeed been admitted to Bletchley. The message was in deep code, of course. But Posie knew what it meant. And naturally it gave none of the details that Alice longed for. Did Louise miss them—at all? What was she doing now with her new face? Had she met anyone? A beau? Was she in the arms of someone who would remember her through a day? A week? Perhaps a lifetime? Would she and her mum and dad ever see Louise again?

Frau Mueller suddenly looked slightly stricken. "Oh, for heaven's sake. I just forgot your name!"

"Ute, Ute Schnaubel."

"Of course." Frau Mueller clapped her hands delightedly. "Silly me."

Stupid you!

"And now, students," Frau Mueller continued. "I would like you to study the sheets that I shall pass out. They show diagrams displaying the differences between Aryans and other races' skulls. You shall see immediately the differences in brain capacity."

Alice was dying to mention Anatole France, one of her mother's favorite French writers, who had published many books and poems. He was known to have an exceptionally small head. But if there was one thing that Alice had learned, it was to keep her thoughts to herself. For Alice . . . or for Ute . . . it was a matter of life or death.

There was no class that was quite as dismal as the racial awareness one. However, the teachers always managed to put a peculiar Nazi twist on everything. Herr Dorfmann welcomed her with a brief explanation of how history was taught: "Fräulein Schnaubel, in this class you shall learn that the purpose of history is to teach young people like yourself that life is always dominated by struggle. At the very center of this struggle are race and blood." His words were almost identical to those of Wilhelm Frick, creator of the Nuremburg Laws that led to the persecution of Jewish people in Germany.

Even in literature, Fräulein Gross managed to describe Shakespeare's melancholy Hamlet as the perfect hero for their times, for his struggle. How she could use the words "resolved" and "resolute" and "fierce" with that dithering prince was unimaginable. But none of this was imaginary. Alice realized that she was sitting in these classes and learning nothing about literature or biology or history. Instead she was dissembling, disguising her true feelings.

An A-level mission was not all about parachuting out of airplanes piloted by handsome young pilots. Nor was it mapping the heavy water plant in Norway, as Louise had done. Spycraft at its highest level required becoming one of "them." Becoming the enemy, becoming a Higher Daughter, and seamlessly blending in.

After school Alice found herself with three of the Higher Daughters, who had invited her to join them at the Bachmann Café, or the Bach, as it was called. Not as fancy as the Café Kranzler across the street, but very nice. She sat between Birgit and Margret, a rather mousy-looking girl, and Lena, a beautiful girl who looked like a younger version of the famous German movie star Marlene Dietrich—except for the pimple on her nose.

"I just can't believe this. It came overnight. Blossomed!" Lena whined.

"Think of it then as a rose!" Birgit said.

"It's not a rose," Margret said. "It's full of pus, and if it fills up any more your nose will get bigger and turn into a Jewish nose."

Alice was sick. She looked at Birgit and Margret. They were giggling at this awful and disgusting "wit." Alice knew she should laugh along with them in order to blend in, but perhaps she could say something else instead.

"Put a hot wet facecloth on it when you get home, and it might pop. Don't squeeze it, though. It might leave a scar." Then she paused. A trace of a smile fled across her face. A joke she could make. "After all, Lena, better a red rose on your nose than a White Rose." All the girls broke out laughing. The White Rose was the name of the resistance movement against Hitler.

"Now that is what I call clever, very clever!" Lena exclaimed. "Thank you, Ute. And the suggestion for the hot cloth is very helpful, and not nasty." She glared at Margret.

Then turned to Alice. "So that is too bad that you have to go through the Jungmädel competitions all over again."

"Oh I don't mind," Alice replied.

"What's your favorite contest? You get to choose, you know."

"I like track. So I'll probably choose that and maybe gymnastics."

"You know Ilse Kranzler?" Margret nodded to the very fancy Café Kranzler across the street. "Yes, those Kranzlers. Well, she's a star gymnast. But not anymore! So you might have a chance." All the girls burst into giggles.

"What's so funny? Why isn't she a star anymore?"

"Because she's pregnant."

"Oh no! And not married or anything?" Now Alice was genuinely shocked.

"Nope," Birgit said. "Ilse would have been your sister guide."

"B-b-b-but. How old is she?"

"Oh, fourteen, maybe almost fifteen."

"And she's having a baby?"

"Yes." Margret nodded solemnly.

"But isn't that too young?"

"A bit," Lena said. "But you know the Führer wants all of us to have babies."

"Not quite *that* young. I know my mum wouldn't like it one bit if I had a baby," Birgit said.

"Nor mine," Lena said.

"Not mine either," Margret said. "But you know, if it happens, it happens."

If it happens, it happens! Alice thought. The conversation was becoming increasingly bizarre. "After all, when we get to be seventeen, we'll be eligible for the Faith and Beauty Society of the girls' league. And just think, Lena, they'll give you all sorts of tips about spots."

Alice glued a benign smile to her face, as if this was all perfectly normal. But really she felt as if she had entered an alternate reality. Still, she joined in, saying, "So you think I might have a good chance for a first medal in gymnastics, now that Ilse Kranzler is out of the running?"

"Definitely!" Margret said. Alice couldn't help but think that things couldn't become any stranger . . . but then they did. "You know, I just had a great idea for my report in RA," Margret said brightly.

"What?" Birgit said.

"I'm going to do my report on earlobes."

"What are you going to say about earlobes?" Lena asked.

"I'm going to start by measuring all your earlobes and sketching them. You know, showing the difference between the hanging earlobe, the creases, and the attached ones. You know, comparing them by race."

"But where will you find other races?" Alice asked. "They've all been locked up."

"My dad has a friend of a friend who works at Ravensbrück. It's not that long a drive from Berlin. I bet he can get me in." Alice squeezed her eyes shut for a moment and tried to imagine this mousy girl going into the women's concentration camp, measuring the prisoners' earlobes. "But if that doesn't work, I can always use photographs and measure."

"But Margret." Alice sighed, trying to conjure up a sympathetic tone. "How are you going to use photographs of the other races?"

"Oh, Frau Mueller has lots of those. You only saw a fraction in her class today."

"Okay, but still," Alice persisted. She noticed a little frown creasing Margret's brow. "How can you compare the measurements of a photo to the measurements you take of our actual ears? I mean, the scale will be different."

The three girls looked at Alice in wonder, as if she was a veritable genius.

"Oh!" Margret inhaled sharply. "Scale. You do have a point. I guess I'll have to think about it."

Yes, thought Alice, *you take that wee brain of yours and have a good think. Idiot.*

But they really aren't idiots, are they?

The question danced through her mind. They were products of this insane culture. They had been brainwashed. How did a person wake herself up from such a brainwashing? How could one hang one's brains out to dry in fresh air? *Watch it, Alice,* she counseled herself. The last thing a spy needed to do was empathize. If she did, it would be her undoing, and in a very short time she would be dead.

"I just want to get high marks," Margret was saying. "If

I do well in the Jungmädel games I might have a chance at an RP."

RP? Alice spun through her memories of all the pages of soft materials she had read. It eluded her. Reich. Reich, that's what the R was for. But Reich what?

"Honestly, Margret, don't take this the wrong way, but I think Jutta Engels has a better chance," Birgit said.

"Not necessarily," Margret snapped.

"I don't think we had the RP in Swabia."

"Oh no! It's only in Berlin. It's the Reich Praktikum. Whoever has the highest grades in both the Jungmädel athletic contests and academics gets a chance to work right in the New Reich Chancellery. You'd have a chance to work in the offices of someone very important—like say Herr Goebbels, the minister of propaganda and enlightenment. Inge Hausmann got to work in the architectural office of Albert Speer."

Alice's eyes opened wide in amazement. She now remembered the mention of this in her soft materials. The words came back to her. *If you perform with consistent excellence, you will become eligible for a part-time position after school in the New Reich Chancellery, the headquarters of the Greater German Reich.*

"Yes, isn't it thrilling?" Margret said. "Just imagine if one of us got such an opportunity."

Alice suddenly knew what her mission was. She was to win the RP, and then be inserted right into the heart of the Reich, under the guise of being a model student. She had no doubt she would win it. Between the Rasas, or the Company, and MI6, the official British secret intelligence service, it would be achieved, even if she didn't qualify.

But she would. After all, she was a Rasa, and endowed with extreme academic talents and athletic ones. Perhaps if the competitions had been in the Beauty and Faith division of the older girls' league, she might have been more challenged. She was no beauty. Besides that, no one could remember her face.

And as for faith? She was just good old Church of England, and that had nothing to do with faith in the god Hitler—she imagined that was what the faith part of that older division was about. Nazis were not particularly concerned with the kinds of faith one practiced at church, except if one went to a synagogue. At the opening assembly of the day, all the students gathered in the auditorium and were required to recite the morning prayer.

Führer, my Führer, given me by God,
Protect and preserve my life for long.
You rescued Germany from its deepest need.
I thank you for my daily bread.
Stay for a long time with me, leave me not.
Führer, my Führer, my faith, my light,
Hail my Führer.

That was the Church of Adolf Hitler. And it frightened Alice to her core.

EIGHT

THE PRINCE OF DARKNESS AND WEASEL HEAD

"So, meine kleine Maus, how did your first day go today with the Higher Daughters of the best school in Berlin?"

"Mum, don't call me your little mouse. One of my classmates is very rodenty looking, though. More rat than mouse, but she's tiny. And mean."

"No, Ute, here's your first lesson for A level. You really never know. Sometimes the meanest in behavior are total cowards. Not to say that they are less dangerous, but they are often less able to act. And the sweetest can be the most deadly and clever. But how did your classes go? And the teachers?"

"Somewhat weird. How about your first day over there?" Alice tipped her head toward the brand-new office buildings where the high command of the German army offices was located. Alice and her mother had met up there after

71

school and were walking back to the Bendlerstrasse garage together. It was actually safer to discuss certain things in a public space. Though the apartment was theoretically clean, there was always the chance that someone could sneak in and plant bugs. Her father checked at least once a day, but one could never be too cautious.

"My day? Well, let's just say working with a bunch of Nazis is not exactly a walk in the park," Posie replied.

"This girl Birgit that I met, she's my sister guide, and her mum works in the same building as you. She's in the race and settlement office."

"What a euphemism for the concentration camps!"

"Mum . . ." Alice slowed her pace and turned toward her mother. "I think I know what my mission is."

Posie's eyebrows seemed to leap like minnows. "I told your father you would catch on immediately."

"I'm to do well in the Jungmädel games on the Führer's birthday and make the highest marks in school. Then I can earn a Reich Praktikum."

"Indeed. It's always better if one uncovers their mission themselves. It means you bring a freshness to it. Unprejudiced."

"Did Louise discover her missions as quickly?"

"Oh, goodness, child, I can't remember. It's not a contest."

Not anymore, thought Alice. Just as she was finally catching up with her sister, Louise had quit the game. Neither Alice nor Posie ever referred to her as Louisa anymore. She was just plain Louise. And although Alice tried to forget her sister's new face, she wasn't very successful. Most times it would simply blend in with her old face in her memories.

"It's always better to let one discover their mission," she said as they walked on. "If we turn here, there's a shortcut to a very good bakery, I'm told. Almost in the Tiergarten, the beautiful park. No flour shortage here yet."

Five minutes later they turned into a narrow street and immediately saw the bakery, Zeiberg Bäckerei.

As soon as they walked through the door, Alice felt as though she was dissolving into a sweet dream of cakes and pastries. There was the scent of anise swirling through the air. "How does one decide?" she gasped.

"Ah, no need to decide, Fräulein. You're welcome to take them all home with you. We have it all—Bienenstiche are our specialty, buttercream with vanilla custard. Yes, we can still get milk and cream. Our cows have not been bombed yet. Just our weapons factories. And so we have our own version of the German bee sting cake. No bees, though. Don't worry. And here, take some of our famous anise cookies—our gift to you. You must be new to the neighborhood, right?"

"Yes, we are," Posie replied.

The man then went behind the counter and began selecting a variety of cookies.

"Danke, das ist aber sehr nett . . . thank you, that is so kind of you, sir," Posie said. "And I shall take one of your bee sting cakes. It looks irresistible with that whipped cream."

"Ah yes," the proprietor replied. "Mit Schlag. What's life without Schlag?"

He put the cake and cookies in a box and handed it across the counter to her as Posie counted out the reichsmarks. "Here you go. I guarantee that you'll be back for more."

And indeed they would be. Each time, Herr Zeiberg thought they were brand-new to the neighborhood and give them a sampling of his best cookies. They did not abuse this privilege, though. They were careful to visit other bakeries as well.

But now, as they walked down Filderstrasse, the smell of the still-warm cookies was so tempting that they each had to have one.

They walked along for a block or two.

"Very fancy neighborhood," Alice said, looking at the grand houses. Many neighborhoods had suffered immeasurable damage from the Allied bombings four months earlier. But this one appeared untouched.

"Oh yes, all these houses near the Tiergarten are owned by wealthy people. It's rather like Kensington or Knightsbridge in London. What a lovely house we had back there on Eaton Square," Posie mused.

"Just two years ago, Mum." They spoke in low voices, even though they were alone on the street.

"Seems longer," her mother replied.

"That's a lovely one, isn't it, Mum? Looks like vanilla custard and with its edges trimmed in whipped cream. Haus mit Schlag." Alice laughed softly.

"I think we can cut down this alley and perhaps see it from the back."

"Oh, let's do it!" Alice said.

They had walked perhaps halfway down the alley when Alice glimpsed a fleeting shadow that seemed to pop out of a garbage bin. She stopped abruptly.

"Why'd you stop?" her mother asked.

"I swear I thought I saw something."

"Something?" her mother asked, scanning the alley.

"I'm not sure. But it was a person, and maybe a child. The person was there and then just vanished. I . . . I think he or she came from that garbage bin."

"You mean out of it? Whoever it is must be very small."

"I don't know, but wait here while I go see."

Alice strode over to the bin. The lid was off. She peered in. Orange rinds, a few champagne bottles, the end of a loaf of bread, a roast chicken just half eaten, four empty caviar jars. *This was a rich person's house,* Alice thought. But had she interrupted someone's dinner—someone who was dining in the garbage bin?

"What are you doing down there?" her mother called from the other end of the alley.

"Just looking."

There was a gate in a wooden fence that must lead to the backyard of the beautiful house—the Whipped Cream House, as she now thought of it. She tried the gate, but it was locked. The cookies were still warm in the box she was holding. Their redolence made her very hungry. She was tempted to eat one right here in the alley. But something stopped her. Was someone watching her? Hungrier than her? She stole a glance at her mother, who was looking at another house across the alley. Putting her hand in the cookie bag, Alice drew one out, then carefully placed it in the bin, between the champagne bottle and the caviar jar.

"Find anything?" her mother asked.

"A rich family's house," she replied. Her mother chuckled. "What's so funny?"

"You know what the very old Rasa term for trash picking was?"

"What do you mean?"

"For what you just did—picking through trash."

"No, what?

"Trash picking . . . sgudail. That's what they called the trash of rich people." She dropped her voice to a bare whisper. "An excellent source for intel."

Oh yes, Alice thought. Now she remembered the head counselor at Rasa summer camp talking about this. Some story from the sixteenth century, when King Henry VIII and the French were fighting. The spymaster himself had lauded the accomplishment of one Rasa on the intelligence he'd uncovered by examining a trash bin near the French king's palace. The golden nuggets of the poubelles. Poubelles was the French word for trash cans. It was such a lovely word for such an unlovely thing.

"Come along. Let's get home with the cake and cookies."

"Yes, of course," Alice replied vaguely, looking back. Whose shadow was that? She could not help but think of Peter Pan, the part where Peter lost his own shadow at the Darlings' house. Nana the dog had snagged it when Peter had leaped from the Darling children's nursery window. That was why Peter returned—to find his shadow. And then Wendy had sewn it back on for him. *How ridiculous,* she thought. A fairy tale at best. And this was not a fairy tale but an A-level mission. She could not be sidetracked by sprinting shadows. Why, then, had she left that cookie?

She must not be distracted. The Jungmädel games were in less than three weeks. She would be practicing gymnastics every day starting tomorrow, and then there was homework too. She found out that the grades from her Swabian school would count. She was unsure how MI6 had arranged this, but she sensed that Count Stauffenberg had taken care of it. She was now certain he must be her fios, and not simply her case manager or contact.

"Yes, Herr Minister, I think the suspension needs adjustment. I drove it around the Tiergarten myself. Can you leave it here tonight? It will be as good as new in the morning."

Another shadow spread across the cement floor of the garage. A shadow that was somewhat askew. It seemed bent, as if it were somehow folding in upon itself. This was Joseph Goebbels, the minister of propaganda. The Winfields had a code name for him: the P of D, or Prince of Darkness. One of the most vicious of all Hitler's ministers.

It was Goebbels who decided the curriculum that would be taught in all the schools. This small man had a mind that was as twisted as his body. He had become the authority on all things Aryan and cultural. He himself had been born with a condition that made his legs uneven in length and caused a severe limp. The irony that he was now the judge of what defined physical perfection seemed to have escaped notice.

Alice knew that he was often called "the dwarf" and that he was at least a head shorter than her father, yet he was no dwarf. He suffered from a clubfoot, for which he had been operated on as a child. The operation was not really successful and only resulted in shortening his right leg dramatically. He was actually about the same height as Alice. But it was his face that stood out—his thin mouth stretched into a peculiar grimace, and he appeared to be almost lipless.

Her father had warned them about Goebbels. It was he who had first called him the Prince of Darkness. In Alan Winfield's mind, he was at the very center of this evil government. Why? Because he knew how to create a deadly infection of hatred among the people and make it spread through his propaganda machine.

"Schönen Tag. Good day, Frau Schnaubel," he said as Alice and her mother returned to the garage with their cake and bag of cookies. Goebbels began lurching toward them. "I see you have discovered the wonderful Zeiberg's bakery. A treasure of the city."

Alice felt her mother clutch her hand. He leaned in for a kiss. She watched his lipless mouth touch each side of her mother's face. Very discreet, very chaste, and very sickening. Her mother's grasp on her hand tightened. "And this must be your daughter, who I've heard so much about."

"Ja," nodded her mother. "This is Ute . . . Ute Maria."

"And you are at the Haupt Gymnasium?"

"Yes, my first day."

"I hope it went well."

"Yes, sir. Very well."

"And you'll be competing in the games on our Führer's birthday."

"Oh yes, sir."

"Joseph," a high-pitched voice trilled. The minister immediately backed away from Alice and her mother. A tall, willowy blond woman swept into the garage. She could have been one of the Rhine maidens from the Wagner operas, one of the nymphs that swirled out of the mists of the river and guarded the gold—except for one small detail.

Alice's eyes settled on the garment wrapped around her shoulders and felt a shudder pass through her as she saw the beady little eyes of a weasel. Frau Goebbels was wearing a tippet, the latest fashion! It was a fur scarf with the paws and head of a small animal—like a weasel—still attached to its pelt. How could a person wear such a thing? But perhaps a glamorous Nazi wife married to the P of D could. A perfect match!

She looked at them both, this almost-royal couple of the Third Reich. He bent on his slightly twisted leg. There was something unnerving about both Goebbels's and his wife's faces. Sharp faces, with chalk-white complexions, and their eyes—his dark, hers a pale gray—had a strange light, glistening and feral. *What a pair,* Alice thought. *The Prince of Darkness and his lovely wife, Weasel Head.*

Goebbels's wife laid a hand on his arm as if to claim him and gave a dark glance toward Posie. "Frau Schnaubel . . . welcome. I see our Berlin food agrees with you." This was not a compliment. "Aach! And you seem to have stopped at my favorite bakery, Zeiberg's!"

"Yes, Frau Goebbels, we couldn't resist."

"I must! I have to resist such temptations, as I must be fit for . . ." She slid her eyes toward her husband. "For Joseph, my lovey."

Alice felt that she was witnessing something most unfit . . . unnatural . . . absolutely sordid. It suddenly dawned on her that again she was up against the true challenge of A-level missions, that of disguising her true feelings and learning to live the lie.

There was more small talk. "I have some homework to do." Alice excused herself from the garage and went up to the apartment and immediately to her small bedroom. She turned on the gramophone and began listening to the Wagner opera *Das Rheingold* for her studies. She felt like she had just witnessed the opening prelude—with the horns suggesting the depth of the Rhine River, as the first of the beautiful maidens emerged from the mists. And then the arrival of the evil dwarf Alberich who craved the gold. A skewed version of that same scene had just played out in the garage. There

80

was the dwarf in the form of Goebbels, and then his wife, Magda, the personification of a Rhine maiden—guarding her gold (in this case her husband).

While Alice listened to the music, she did several math problems for the next day and then completed a horrible homework exercise that asked her to construct her own racial family tree.

She began with this sentence. "The Schnaubel family dates back to the late fourteenth century in Swabia. The first recorded Schnaubel was a cobbler in the town of Tannheim. On my mother's side, her maiden name was Olsen. On the racial complexion chart, my mother's skin registers as a 1.1 in terms of fairness. And my father is a 1.2."

To complete the exercise, she was required to fill in other information, or "data," as Frau Mueller referred to it. It was Frau Mueller herself who had devised this exercise, and she had been commended by the department of education for it. It was to be adopted for other biology and racial awareness classes throughout Berlin.

Alice clamped her eyes shut. She realized that she had entered the twilight world of evil, and at its very center was the dark heart of hatred. A hatred that was seeping through everything good, everything honorable. This was to be her mission now. Her war. To find out the secrets of this evil Nazi regime and report them to His Majesty's secret service.

She stood up from her desk and went to her closet to get her gym tunic. She could take no chances. She must win the games. At Haupt they had all the gymnastic equipment—the balance beams, the mats. They even had a running track. But she needed to build her endurance. She must start running every day now.

She dressed and went into the dining room, where her mother had just put dinner on the table. Her parents greeted her with a slightly astonished look.

"Where are you going dressed like that at this time of the evening?"

"For a run. It's still light out." She paused. "I can't take any chances on not winning."

Her parents exchanged quick glances. They agreed. Nothing needed to be said. The word "mission" did not even need to be articulated. Rasa families were not mind readers, but they could say much without ever speaking aloud.

From that moment on, every morning and every evening Alice ran. That first evening she could only manage three miles, but by the end of the week she was doing five miles in the evening and three in the morning. In the gym at school, she quickly distinguished herself as someone to watch, especially in the broad jump.

Nevertheless, even Frau Grauber, the gymnastics coach, often had trouble placing her face when she walked into the gym. But finally it would dawn on her. This girl was the air sprite! "Ah, meine kleine Luftelfe!" she would exclaim. My little air sprite. "You sprint like a shadow!"

NINE

SHADOW PLAY

Like a shadow. The words thrummed in her head, coursed through her bloodstream as she ran the short distance to the Tiergarten. Entering the park, she always breathed a sigh of relief. It was as if she had left the evil behind. How could hatred prevail here in this glade of burgeoning greenness of early spring? The late afternoon sun fell like streams of liquid light through the canopy of trees. She accelerated. It was a seemingly endless park, verdant with winding tree-lined paths and broad open spaces. It seemed evil could not touch this place, and yet her teacher Frau Grauber's words haunted her. *You sprint like a shadow!*

There was another shadow that she could not banish from her mind. For almost two weeks she had avoided the vanilla-custard house trimmed in whipped cream, the Haus mit Schlag, and the alley behind it, where that other shadow had sprinted. She stopped short now. She knew she had to turn back. The bakery would still be open. She could buy another cookie, but first she would have to go back for some money.

"Back so soon?" her mother called out.

"I . . . uh . . . had a craving for some of those cookies. The anise ones."

"I was just in there this morning. But I didn't buy cookies."

"Did he remember you?"

"Of course not. I've been in there at least three times now. Never even a glimmer of recognition. Each time he welcomes me and gives me something free. I feel guilty now. He's given me too much."

"Well, not me. I really love those cookies."

"All right, run along."

Ten minutes later she walked into the shop. She stopped short. There was a new scent, and it was not anise, nor anything that went into a cookie or a cake. It was perfume. And not just any perfume, but Laurel Bright, the perfume that Louise sometimes wore. An inexpensive British perfume. One could buy it at the chemist. But why would that scent be trailing through the Zeiberg bakery? Alice felt momentarily disoriented.

"Aah." Herr Zeiberg greeted her with delight. "You new to the neighborhood?"

"Uh . . . yes, more or less. Just out for a run." She sniffed. Immediately she knew she shouldn't have. But she felt completely discombobulated. This would not do. Spies could not feel discombobulated, flummoxed, or anything else.

"Oh, practicing for Jungmädel games?"

"Yes, sir," she answered crisply.

"My daughter too. So what can I do for you?"

"Ah . . . some of those cookies maybe—the anise ones?" she said, pointing to the glass case.

"Of course, but let me get you some kleine Kuchen for you as well—fresh out of the oven." He went through a door and came back a few seconds later with a tray of hot little cakes.

"Thank you, sir. How much do I owe you?"

"Nothing. A welcome gift. Pick out some cookies too." As he was packing up the cookies and cakes, the bell on the door jingled, announcing a new customer.

"Ah, Frau Goebbels, what a treat to see you again. How is the minister?"

"Gut . . . gut . . . never better."

Alice froze. Would the woman recognize her? Her tunic had the name of her school. She knew that Frau Goebbels's husband had finally recognized her father, but never outside the garage. That was usually how it worked. A Rasa was most often recognized when he or she was in the context of their own workplace. Five minutes after that, a Rasa could be in the street and the person would not recall having seen them. At most, the person might think, if they bumped into each other, that perhaps he or she had met them some time before but couldn't identify where or when. The Rasa would be just a vaguely familiar face.

Alice turned now to leave, trying her best to avoid a direct confrontation, but just at that moment Magda's attention was drawn to her by the fragrance of the freshly baked little cakes.

"Ummm! That smells divine. What have you got there, dear?"

"Uh . . . just some cakes, kleine Kuchen . . . ," Alice answered.

"May I have a peek?"

"Of course." What could she do? She set the box on the counter. Her hands were trembling as she untied the box. She tried to smile. Frau Goebbels sniffed the open box. She raised her head and looked Alice directly in the face. *Weasel head!*

"Lovely, I think I'll ask for some myself, Herr Zeiberg." Then she turned back to Alice. "Thank you, child. What pretty blue eyes you have. And I think you look just a little bit like that very young actress Elizabeth Taylor. I just came from the cinema. That wonderful film *Lassie Come Home*. Her hair is very black, almost like a Jewish child's 's hair, but her eyes are nearly violet. Yes, really like Elizabeth Taylor. I believe she is about your age."

"Yes, madame. I mean, I don't know how old she is. But I hear she is a very pretty."

Clutching her bag of cookies and her box of little cakes

to her chest, Alice dashed out the door. Between the scent of the perfume and the encounter with Frau Goebbels, she was more than agitated.

Frau Goebbels was real, but the scent of that perfume could not have been real. Did they sell that perfume here in Germany? She stopped for a moment and shut her eyes. Her mind spun backward. It was as if she was watching a movie in reverse—the frames flashing backward. The sound of the mirror shattering in their cottage back in England when Louise furiously slammed the door. Then the preceding frame in the film—the argument that had started when she'd come across Louise primping in the mirror, dabbing on the new perfume. The harsh exchange with their words cutting like glass fragments: . . . *one question before you slam me out . . . You're being dramatic . . . Am I now? Oh, that's rich . . . I think you're the dramatic one. You look like an actress trying out expressions for an audition. . . .*

Alice knew she had to push all these thoughts out of her mind—the words, the scent. It was ridiculous. More than one person could wear that scent. It wasn't as if it was Chanel No. 5. It was cheap. Chemists carried it. You could buy it if you went in to buy a packet of gum, Band-Aids, cough syrup, and yes, a bottle of Laurel Bright, please. It cost less than a pound. A few shillings, maybe. Countless women might be wearing that scent. She was just being foolish. It was a needless distraction. And needless distractions had no place in the superior minds of Rasa spies.

She had something more important to do. Sgudail. Yes, the old Rasa term her mum had used. Trash picking . . . considered an excellent source of intel. She needed to deliver these cakes and cookies to . . . to . . . the shadow . . . lurking in the rich people's garbage.

Taking the shortest route to the whipped-cream house, she stopped suddenly on the corner diagonally across from it. A very official-looking auto had just pulled up in front of the mansion. The door opened and a man stepped out. Alice inhaled sharply. He wore the gray-green uniform of the SS, the Schutzstaffel, which was the military unit charged with enforcing Hitler's racial policies.

And this man was no mere officer. There was a scramble of gold brocade on the shoulder boards of his uniform indicating that he was a general, and not simply any general. The oak leaves on the notched lapels meant he was an SS Oberstgruppenführer, a highest-command general. No wonder there were all those champagne bottles and caviar jars in the trash bins. But how did that explain the shadow? Who was the shadow, and where had it come from?

Dare she creep into the alley now and leave the cookies in the bin? Her own shadow was lengthening. She waited until the general entered the house and the government auto pulled away, then began to walk calmly toward the alley. She had the oddest feeling that she was being watched. Was the shadow near?

The trees that bordered the backyards of the houses

rustled in a light breeze. Their leaves seemed to whisper to her, beckoning her. She realized that she had begun to tiptoe down the alley. How ridiculous! Tiptoeing in her gym shoes toward the trash bin. She looked around and, as quietly as possible, removed the cover from the bin and put the entire bag of cookies and the box of small cakes on top of some coffee grounds. There was a moment, as she placed the bag and box, that she actually thought she could feel the shadow's hunger. She almost heard a gasp, but it was just the shiver of the linden trees' leaves in the breeze. Replacing the lid as quietly as possible, she hurried away to the corner of the alley.

She decided to wait to see what might happen. Would the shadow appear? She was uncertain if he—or possibly she—might be glimpsed. She walked a few steps to a larger bin, which she could crouch behind and peek out. She could see various lights begin to flick on in the whipped-cream house. She figured that the kitchen in the house was downstairs, on the basement level. This was often the case in these large mansions. As much space as possible was put between the kitchen and the dining area, as servants were to be rarely seen. Food was delivered on dumbwaiters to the upstairs pantry, and the staff of butlers and footmen would then serve.

She was enormously curious about this house. If she were up higher she might be able to peek over the wall. There was a low branch in almost full foliage that hung over the bin. Dared she try and get to it from the top of the bin and then into the tree? If she could, she would have an excellent vantage point and be camouflaged by its leaves. She was atop the bin in two seconds and in another three had swung herself onto the branch—as easily as jumping onto the balance beam for gymnastics. She decided to climb higher, to the leafiest part of the tree.

Nimble as a lemur, she ascended the tree. Then, tucked into this green cubbyhole between alley and sky, Alice peeked over the adjoining fences that separated the backyards of the houses from the alley. She was peering down on a lovely terraced garden. Tulips were in bloom, and there was a small pond that flashed with goldfish swimming. Pots spilled with pansies and ivy, and honeysuckle blossoms clambered up a trellis. On another trellis was a cascade of frothy tiny white flowers. It was a fairyland. She could almost imagine that she had been transported back to England, to Misselthwaite and to her favorite book, *The Secret Garden*. How she had loved that book, and the garden that Mary and Dickon brought back to life, and Colin, Mary's sickly cousin, who Mary also brought back to life in her own way.

She now saw a corpulent woman lumber across the garden of the whipped-cream house with two large bags of garbage. The woman pushed through the back gate. Setting the bags down, she removed the bin's lid. Alice saw her head jerk slightly; then she leaned forward and peered deeper into the bin.

"*Was ist das?*" she heard the woman mutter as she drew out the bag of cookies.

No . . . no . . . no . . ., Alice thought. The woman took out a cookie, looked at it, then bit into it.

"Ummm," she hummed, and licked her lips. *"Warum sollte jemand einen Keks wegwerfen, der noch völlig in Ordnung ist?"* Why would someone throw away a perfectly good cookie?

"Because," Alice mumbled to herself, "someone else is starving near here." *The shadow!*

Alice knew it, and she was determined to feed that shadow.

At just that moment, she heard a slight rustle in the tree across from her. She gasped as she saw the dark eyes of a painfully thin boy peering directly at her. He put a finger to his lips and then vanished. *Colin?* she wondered. From *The Secret Garden?*

TEN

HAPPY BIRTHDAY, DEAR FÜHRER!

On the day of the Jungmädel competition, Alice woke up
with a start. That scent again! Had she been dreaming?
Could dreams have scents? It was not real. She knew this.
For there was another scent that seeped up now from the
garage below. There had been a big motor oil spill the evening before, and a thick carpet of sawdust had been laid
down to soak it up. The pungent wood odor mixed with that
of the oil was distinct and permeated their living quarters.
No way could Laurel Bright cut through that odor. Since that
day nearly three weeks ago, she'd successfully banished any
distracting thoughts of that strange scent she'd encountered
in the bakery and convinced herself that it been a product of
her imagination.

Perhaps, she reasoned, she had felt such deep remorse over

the harsh words she had spoken to her sister, Louise, that it was in some way connected to that. Maybe she wanted to apologize. The times they had made up in the past after squabbling were always so nice. They would think of something fun to do—almost like a celebration. They'd go out for ice cream or their mum would lend them money for a cream tea or to go to the cinema. That must be what she was feeling when she smelled that fragrance. It was nothing more than wishful thinking.

She heard a canon go off outside. April 20, Adolf Hitler's birthday and the official start of his birthday celebration. She had to get dressed quickly, for she would be marching in the parade as a competitor in the Jungmädel events.

There were tanks and flyovers by at least three units of fighter planes. Thousands of goose-stepping soldiers followed by more than a dozen Jungmädel competitors, as well as the older girls from the Bund Deutscher Mädel of the German Girls' League. These athletic events were held all over Berlin. The events that Alice would be competing in were at a stadium called the Little Handelsblatt, in the Mitte district of Berlin.

And three hours later she swung onto the balance beam dressed in her black shorts and white sleeveless T-shirt with the emblazoned Nazi Eagle. She hadn't planned to compete in this exercise, but when Elske Meyers sprained her ankle, Fräulein Grauber had begged her to compete. She had said she would, though track was more her strength than gymnastics.

"Do both, Ute. There are ten days until the games. You can practice. I'll stay after school and coach you. I'll get you excused from music during the day. You are just as good as Elske. Maybe even better. Please, Ute, do it. Do it for me. . . . No! Do it for the Führer, like a good Jungmädel!"

Alice had nodded and agreed, for the Führer. This was what one did as a Rasa. One lied, one acted, one performed for God, king, and country—England, not Germany. And no one would ever suspect. Because she, Alice Winfield, was a member of the most skilled intelligence service on earth. And so now, at the Little Handelsblatt stadium, she sprinted out from the bench and lofted herself in one smooth leap onto the balance beam.

For the past two weeks, though, she had been able to think of nothing else but the shadow boy. Every day she had managed to drop off food. She was careful to make sure that the housemaid had finished filling up the bin and would not be coming out. But just last night the bin had been empty, and she was uncertain what to do. She had brought a baked potato and a slice of cake, neatly tied up in a cloth. She didn't want to put it in the empty bin for fear the housemaid would find it. So instead she put it in another house's trash bin that was already full. She sensed that the shadow boy was watching. She certainly hoped he was.

She planned to go back there as soon as she was free from the competition. But that would be another few hours. She must push such thoughts out of her mind and concentrate now. She walked forward on tiptoes, then back. She pivoted and then suddenly exploded into a split leap, followed by a scissor leap. She finished with a series of handsprings, culminating in a backflip with a twist.

She did not win, but she placed second. With a first in the track events, she was likely to be eligible to become a candidate for Highest Service to the Reich, or Höchster Dienst am Reich. HDR, as such girls were called. This was not the same, however, as being a Fount of Life girl. Only girls from the older division were eligible for that, *thank god!* Alice thought. Of course, her parents would never permit her to do that, even if she were old enough. These girls were selected because of their perfect racial hygiene for the Lebensborn program. The aim of the program was to increase the birth rate of Aryan children for the nation. The government provided financial support to unmarried women at the maternity homes.

But as an HDR girl—well, an infinite number of possibilities would open up, and it would help her mission to win the RP, the Reich Praktikum. And then she could come closer to the inner circles of the Reich itself. Her mother was now in the typists' pool and had already cracked a low-level code often embedded in what might appear to be a casual memo.

It was what her mum called the Danke Code. It seemed that in a scattering of ordinary letters, one officer at the OKW was often thanking another for remembering his wife's birthday or sending a fruit basket or tickets to the opera. But it was really a code for troop movements or messages about U-boats often dispatched across the Atlantic Ocean toward the northeast coast of Maine. It had nothing to do with flowers or opera tickets. It was invaluable intelligence.

"And now, ladies and gentlemen, we have calculated the scores of the participants today with their academic records and shall ask the recipients of Highest Service to the Reich to step forward and receive their certificates from Lieutenant Colonel Werner Grothmann." There was a wild cheer from the audience. Grothmann was the aide to none other than Heinrich Himmler, the architect of the Jewish extermination program—the Final Solution, as it was called.

Grothmann was a handsome man with slicked-back blond hair and a squarish jaw. He was often in the offices where Alice's mother worked. She said the young women swooned over him. They called him Gary Cooper, after the famous American movie star. He began to read the names of the girls.

"Brünnhilde Achmann, Inge Bretzman, Gerta Hammacher, Erika Hunnolz . . ."

People applauded. The parents stood up and yelled and often hugged each other for producing such fine Aryan specimens of physical prowess and intelligence. The names were in alphabetical order, so Schnaubel was the thirtieth to be announced. Her parents leaped up like the rest when her name was called, rejoicing that their own daughter was among the elite of these racially pure, extraordinary young girls. They even had tears in their eyes. They were, of course, the consummate spies.

Lotte Schnaubel, or Posie Winfield, had just had another success herself. Four VIIC U-boats had been redirected from the north, in Brest, France, just in the nick of time. They had been heading toward the Bay of Biscay, on a search mission for two British anti-submarine ships. But because of Posie's intelligence, the British ships were able to get out of harm's way.

As Alice mounted the stairs to receive her certificate, she saw the lieutenant colonel smile broadly at her as she approached. He grasped her hand warmly and leaned forward. His ice-gray eyes twinkled a bit. "My, what a pleasure it is to shake your hand, Fräulein. You have lovely brown eyes, just like my favorite niece." Her eyes were not brown, of course. But when he looked at her face, which seemed so lacking in any distinctive feature, he simply superimposed what came to mind. Two seconds later he said, "I just attended her fifth birthday party yesterday." For Alice it just meant that another person had projected a convenient face onto her own.

When the ceremony concluded, Alice and her parents began walking from the stadium to their apartment over the garage. Alice wore a blue flower pinned to her tunic, a symbol of her exalted status now as an HDR girl. A Reich heroine. Perfect strangers came up to congratulate her.

The family stopped in at another bakery, as her mother wanted to get a Linzer torte to celebrate. But the baker refused payment. "An HDR girl—never! I bow down before you." He made a sweeping gesture. Her father mildly protested. But the baker would hear nothing of it.

"And I detect a slight Swabian accent. I insist that you take some of our Hefezopf loaves, fresh out of the oven. I make miniature ones. I'll give you a half dozen."

"Oh no, you are too kind," Posie said.

"Nonsense, madame. One cannot be too kind. Our very own daughter is now a Fount of Life mother, and about to give birth any day." Alice felt something seize up in her. She and her parents thought that this breeding program was one of the foulest of the regime. It was only outdone by the extreme evil of the extermination measures that sent Jewish people to their deaths at concentration camps. But her mother smiled tightly and said only, "I wish her and the baby good health."

"What else could it be but good health? No defects in our family for countless generations." Sheer delight danced in his eyes as he spoke.

They walked out of the store with their baked goods.

"I'll never touch his damn sweets," her mother muttered. She began walking toward a trash bin.

"You can't, Lotte. It's too much of a waste." They always addressed one another by their cover names in public.

"We're going to that reception tonight. Won't be home

until later. We won't need to stuff ourselves when we get home," her mother said.

"But I'm home!" Alice replied. "I don't want to have to wait until you get home to eat."

"Yes, and I made you some chicken."

Aaah, she thought. *I'll have a feast to bring to Tree Boy.*

He was no longer the shadow but had become the boy in the tree. She was almost desperate to get back to the alley and see if he had picked up the little cakes she had put in the other garbage bin the day before. She could take a few of the Hefezopf, and perhaps one of the hard-boiled eggs her mother had put aside. Alice liked to imagine the boy eating these treasures and growing fatter. She thought of him constantly now.

ELEVEN
TREE BOY

With two small loaves, still warm, two eggs, an orange, and a quarter of a roasted chicken in her knapsack, Alice made her way toward the whipped-cream house. She stopped at the corner before turning into the alley. A black Mercedes-Benz automobile was pulled up in front of the mansion. She felt a chill run through her. It was another SS vehicle. The insignia was on its license plate.

Two officers stepped out. Alice gasped. Exactly two hours before, she had shaken the hand of the first man, Werner Grothmann. And the second man was Heinrich Himmler. She recognized him from the garage. Her father had worked on his car, this very Mercedes. But why were they coming to this house?

Did one of them live here? She hated to think of either one

of these two loathsome creatures living in this lovely house with the magical garden in the back. She walked around the alley.

"Hey there!" A voice cracked the air. Alice froze in her footsteps. "Yes, you. Might you come over here for just a minute?" She turned and walked back to where the two men stood.

"This is the Schmelling house, is it not?" It was Himmler who asked the question, but Werner Grothmann was looking at her. Would he remember her? At least she had changed out of her tunic and was no longer wearing the blue flower.

"I . . . I . . . I'm not sure," she replied. "I don't live in this neighborhood." She thought fast. She had run so many times through the Tiergarten, weaving in and out of the bordering streets, that the map of the district was etched in her brain. "I live over on Leberstrasse and was just cutting through. I'm sorry."

"Ach! No problem." Grothmann gave a chuckle. He looked straight into her face with complete blankness in his eyes. She walked away and then cut into the alley. She wouldn't be frightened off so easily. She needed to leave this feast for the boy. In her mind, he had become like the boy Colin from *The Secret Garden*—in need of her support.

She put the food in the trash bin. It was full. There was no danger of the housemaid coming out with more bags to put in. They would never fit.

Once again, she felt his presence. She knew he was

watching. What if she climbed the tree? Might she see him again? It was worth a try.

Within less than a minute she was looking down from her perch at the garden that seemed exceptionally beautiful. She heard the back door slam. Was the maid coming out now? *Oh, please don't let her find the food!* she prayed. This was the most she had ever left, and probably the healthiest. But no. It was not the maid. It was three gentleman officers of the SS. Heinrich Himmler, the man responsible for the concentration camps, as well as his assistant, Werner Grothmann, and a third who must live in the house, SS Officer Schmelling. The three oak leaves on his collar indicated a very high rank, that of an Oberstgruppenführer; in short, the supreme group leader, almost if not equal to Himmler. She knew Schmelling was in charge of the military police units that rounded up the Jews for transport to the camps. That was handled by part of her mother's group within the general army's office.

She now noticed a bottle of champagne on a small round table with a lacy cloth covering. The men took a seat. The door opened again, and an older woman in a black dress wearing a starched apron and a white scalloped collar came out with a tray of hors d'oeuvres. She set down the tray and left. Himmler stood and picked up the champagne bottle.

"A toast, gentlemen." He began to uncork the bottle of champagne. "News today from the commandant of Auschwitz. Rudolf Hess reports that the Zyklon B is proving itself most efficient, as are the gas chambers themselves. As of a few days ago, up to six thousand Jews, Romá, and homo-sexuals are being exterminated each day. The infestation of vermin is being vanquished. Purity is being restored—every minute of every single day."

The cork popped loudly and sailed into the air. Alice felt nausea sweep through her as she perched in the tree. The leaves above her shivered as the cork dropped through the green canopy and landed directly in her lap. She picked it up and looked at it, then shifted her gaze to the tree across from her. Her breath caught in her throat. He was there! The shadow boy. The tree boy! A lost boy. Tears rolled down his face. She pointed down toward the trash bin. He nodded.

It was as if they didn't need words. A silent agreement was made. They would both stay in their trees as long as it took for the men to go back into the house. Then they would meet. Alice felt a strange sort of excitement pass through her, as if she was on the precipice of an adventure that had nothing to do with her mission. A boy who lived in trees was about to perhaps become her friend. There was something almost magical about it.

Was he a changeling of some sort? How she had loved all those changeling tales when she was very young. Stories were told of a changeling child left in the place of a real child by fairies. They were stories that had made her weep. Weep for both children, the real one and the fairy child. The illustra-tions in the picture books always made the children look frail, both young and old at the same time—as if they had seen too much in their short lives, and yet had gained an unnatural kind of wisdom. In fact, their faces and eyes seemed almost luminous with this strange kind of knowledge.

Alice and the tree boy did not fall asleep. They did not grow tired.

The light dwindled, the stars broke out. She knew her parents wouldn't miss her, as they had the reception and would be home long after dinner. At one point the maid came out with a painting and held it up so the other two men could see.

"A Jewish painter?" Himmler asked as he looked at the landscape.

"I don't think so," Schmelling replied. "Egon Schiele. Austrian. Died more than twenty years ago. Worth quite a bit, I'm told."

The men drank another bottle of champagne and another, and then began to drink schnapps. They were reeling by the time they walked back into the house. Alice and the boy heard the door slam, and then within three minutes or so the sound of the Mercedes-Benz on the street started up. Alice was sure it was Himmler's car. She knew the sound of a Mercedes, as opposed to, say, a Daimler.

She knew these sounds well, just as she had learned the racketing noise of the Heinkel bombers and the Messerschmitt fighter planes that had carpeted the skies over England two years ago. Like most Rasas, she had developed a sonographic memory. It was the reason they all learned languages so quickly, with just the right intonations for any accent or dialect. Similarly, she knew the sound of a loose fuel injector pump. This one had it. Her father had described it as the sound of an asthmatic sparrow, a slightly wheezing noise. Himmler's Mercedes would be back in her dad's shop in a couple of days.

She looked at the boy. He held up his hand and spread his fingers. Was this a signal that they should wait five minutes? Within about three minutes he was climbing down the tree, and then he began to climb up the one where she sat.

TWELVE
GOD WOULD EAT A PIG

"My name is David," he said as he swung up onto the branch beside her. With anyone else, Alice might have worried that the branch would break. But it was as if a small bird had alighted from the sky. The limb hardly registered his weight.

"I'm Ute."

"Thank you, Ute." The name sounded so wrong in her ears. She desperately wanted to tell him her real name. *The true me!* Louise's words exploded in her head.

"No need to thank me. You're hungry." *But why?* she wanted to ask.

"You won't tell anybody, will you?"

"No! Why would I ever tell someone that you're hungry?" But the truth was slowly dawning on her. The tears, the house, the small gasp he had emitted when the maid brought out the painting. Alice tipped her head toward the whipped-cream house. "You lived there, didn't you?"

He nodded and looked down. In barely a whisper, he spoke. "I lived there with my parents. It was our house and so was the painting. The Nazis took the house. I live there now. But they don't know it."

"How can that be?"

He lifted his head and his eyes sparkled. "Because I'm a clever lad."

"Tell me!" Alice said. "Tell me." She leaned closer to him. "And the garden. Tell me about this beautiful garden."

"My mother designed it. Planted it. Next to music, that was her passion—gardening, flowers, making things grow. There is a wild part that you cannot see. It is my favorite part of the garden. Thick with ferns and woodland flowers—like lady's slippers, and woodland phlox with blossoms like stars. Truly a heaven on earth."

"It sounds like a fairy tale."

"It was, once upon a time." His eyes turned dreamy. "My mother, my papa, and my sister, Ellie, lived in this house and this garden. My papa was a doctor. My mother was a musician, a pianist. And we . . . we . . . Ellie and me were just children."

He spoke these words in such a wistful way, but when he uttered the words "just children," it was as if some strange alchemy occurred and he instantly looked like a little old man.

"Ellie was just a toddler. Now she would be . . ." He shook his head and sighed. "I seem to lose track of time, but now she would be almost four. I was eight. Just children. Baby Ellie was . . ." His voice broke. Tears began to leak from his eyes. With his fist, he wiped snot from his nose—the way any kid would. Except he was not any kid.

"You see, a notice was given that we, like all the Jews in the city, were to report to a deportation center. Ours was on Levetzowstrasse. Not far from our synagogue. We went. We lined up. We were told that we would be going to Lodz, or possibly Riga. All cities that would welcome us. So they told my father. On the day we were to report, we went. There was no way we could not go, especially in this neighborhood, as they sent special squads of SS to take us to the deportation centers. That man you saw in our garden—Schmelling. He loved the house. When he walked in he was exclaiming constantly, 'What an elegant place! How could vermin be here?' He meant us—a Jewish family.

"My father could not hold back. He stepped forward and said, 'High Colonel Schmelling, are you by any chance related to Ernst Schmelling?'

"'Indeed, he's my father,' the colonel replied.

"'I am Dr. Bloom, and I believe I repaired a myocardial laceration your father had suffered—a direct suture. One of the first of this kind of heart surgery,'" David continued. "But this got us nowhere. Schmelling wanted our house. And so we were delivered to the deportation station, along with our neighbors, the Goldsteins and the Cohns. There were hundreds, maybe thousands, of people there. I could see my father growing desperate. Mother was holding Ellie and my father was grasping my hand so tightly, but suddenly he dropped it. He dipped into his pocket and took out a wad of paper money, reichsmarks—large denominations. My father told me to turn my jacket inside out so the star wouldn't show and to go to the butcher on the corner of Haffenstrasse, by the flower shop, and buy bread and sausage. 'Make sure it's pork,' he whispered.

"'B-b-but . . . but . . . I might not find you when I come back.'

"'Don't worry,' he said. 'I'll be right here.'

"But of course he wasn't. By the time I came back, the street was empty. Everyone had vanished. They had been put on a transport train." He paused a long time. "And now I know why he told me to buy pork. Nobody would believe I was Jewish if I had pork sausage on me."

"So that was the last you saw of your father?"

"Yes. I became an instant orphan. And almost instantly stopped keeping kosher. Oh, I tried not to eat the sausage. That lasted all of maybe a day and one night. But then I decided God wouldn't care." He paused a moment. "No, actually that's not quite right. God would care. That's why we were created. God means for us to live." He paused. "And you know something? If he thought it would save one child, God would eat a pig."

109

Alice remained silent for nearly a minute. As a child of Rasas, she had heard a lot of incredible stories, but this was beyond anything. "But I don't understand. How can you live in that house? You said you did." David nodded. "But without them knowing?"

"I only started living there recently. For a long time, I hid out in friends' houses. They were good to me. Many had known my father, as he had been their doctor. I remembered some of their names. And then my mother had taught music to a few as well. But it became too dangerous for them to hide me. So early last winter I moved back in here."

Alice blinked. "But how can you? How can you live right under Reichsführer Schmelling's nose?"

"I remembered a room—well, not really a room, but a secret space. It's behind a panel in the cellar of the house. On most nights, very late, I can get there. It's warm."

"How do you get in?"

"The window well."

"Window well?"

"At the base of the house there is a dugout spot. I'm sure you've seen them. They put a window right on top of the foundation of the house so light can come in if someone needs to go to the cellar. That's how I get in. The glass is broken. It was repaired, but just temporarily with some plywood. Very easy to remove."

"But you don't stay down there all the time, I guess."

"No, the hidden space is so small I can't lie down in it

or stand up. Barely sit up. I just sleep there on really cold nights."

"And on other nights?"

"Oh, I just ramble around. The Tiergarten is good. But the best trash—the best food is in the garbage bins in this alley. Gourmet eating, I tell you."

"What about real gourmet restaurants? They must have great garbage bins full of fantastic food."

"Too much competition. Every street kid, beggar, whatever, is eating out of those bins. The Orpo is always patrolling those places."

Alice knew about the Orpo. It was short for the Ordnungspolizei, or the green police, as they were often called because of their green uniforms.

"Thugs, the whole lot. Every Orpo is hoping to get to be in the secret police, the Gestapo. That makes them extra brutal. Imagine wanting to grow up to be a thug in a green uniform. Not me!" he said, and laughed harshly.

Alice had never thought of herself as an impulsive person, but she suddenly blurted out, "Then what do you want to be when you grow up?"

A smile broke over David Bloom's face. A kind of unnameable joy spilled from his eyes.

"Ute, you really think I can grow up?"

THIRTEEN

A SUNFLOWER BLOOMS

Her parents were still out when Alice returned. She was tired and went straight to bed. But she could not fall asleep. She was haunted by David Bloom. His story of escape and survival haunted her. How had he done it? He had been barely eight years old when his father sent him off with the money for the pork sausage, and now he was just ten—three years younger than she was. She could not help but wonder how quickly her face would fade from his memory.

Now, after more than a month in the Haupt school, people were beginning to know her a bit. But if they were out of school—out of context, was the Rasa phrase—they hardly ever recalled her name. Just yesterday she had been going into a shop for her mother, and she ran into Birgit and her mother. Birgit, her Schwesterführerin, sister guide, did not recall her at all!

If Alice and David encountered each other outside the alley—outside the tree, for that matter—would he remember her? What if they encountered each other in the Tiergarten, where she liked to run? What would happen then?

She yawned. But still sleep was far away. Soon, very soon, the details of her role would come through. For she had now officially qualified as an RP, a Reich Praktikum student of the Jungmädel—one of two from the elite Hermann von Haupt school. She couldn't sleep. She was very excited about the role that would soon be revealed to her. She was equally curious as to who her fios, her mission contact, would be. She felt certain it must be Stauffenberg.

The code name for her fios was Wotan. In one version of the old Norse myth, Wotan's name was Odin, and Odin had only one eye. It was so obvious to her now. Why had she never thought of it? When they had first met, she had wondered if he would be wearing an eye patch or have one of those eerie glass eyes. And she had worried about how one could shake hands with a man who only had one hand with three fingers remaining. She'd met many men and woman who came to the garage. There were the chauffeurs of men high in the government. But not all were official government people. Even the famous and very beautiful Leni Riefenstahl, the Führer's favorite filmmaker, had brought in her Daimler. Yet not one of those people could she imagine betraying the Führer by being her fios.

But she wondered not only about her fios, but her brush contact—would Stauffenberg be that too? Brush contacts

113

were very important, as they provided a method for two seeming strangers to pass each other on the street and exchange, through a single word or a scrap of paper, vital information. And she hadn't yet received any instructions about dead drops, as they were called, secret locations where she could leave urgent encoded information. Nor did she know the signal spots where she could make her chalk marks if she needed to contact her fios or other agents in the spy circle.

These were methods that they had all practiced at Rasa camp in Scotland. She knew the tricks well. She had been quite proficient with the brush contacts, but you never really knew until you did it for real. It wasn't like a parachute practice jump—if you landed wrong, you could break a leg or an arm. Instant feedback. But dead drops and brush byes were different.

Alice's thoughts turned to the very first Rasas, the ones from almost four hundred years ago, in the time of Henry VIII. None of these methods had been invented then, or if they had, they were in their infancy. Every Rasa child at some time during summer camp read the diary of William Morfitt to learn the Rasa history. And then on Morfitt's birthday, August 18, portions were always read aloud.

As I sit here tonight on the eve of my eighty-eighth birthday— nearly a century old—it is difficult to believe that it has been sixty-eight years since I began my service in the court.

I started as a groom of the stool in the court of Henry VIII's father, when Henry VIII was still married to Catherine of Aragon. Groom of the stool is a rather elegant title for an inelegant position—one who attends to the king's bodily functions. In short, shit and piss.

The campers always giggled about the rude language.

At Rasa camp, a play was always performed on the night before Sir William's birthday. It was based on his time as a spy when Morfitt had actually been caught for spying and imprisoned in France. This was the second time Morfitt had been aided by a person whose face he simply could never remember, even though they had provided crucial help for him.

Because Alice had received such a high score in her language studies and had mastered the dialect of northern Brittany in France, she played the role of the woman who helped Morfitt escape. "Ha deuit ganin." Follow me, monsieur.

She wondered if any of her fellow campers had received an A-level mission yet. Most likely they had, as this was war. The most dangerous war in the history of the United Kingdom. She recalled that her friend Peter Jenkins had been dispatched to someplace in North Africa. He had picked up Arabic quickly and had mastered a range of dialects.

She heard the front door of the apartment open and close.

Her parents must be home. Less than a minute later, there was a light tapping on her door.

"Ja."

"Noch wach?" her mother asked. Still awake?

"Ja, Mutter, herein." The German word "Mutter," for Mother, was not nearly as cozy as Mum. But it was necessary that they speak only German.

"Haushaltsdienst," her mother said. Housekeeping services.

Alice whistled softly. So she was to be in domestic service of the Reich. One could not get much closer to the center of things. It was the very belly of the beast—Hitler's houses and apartments.

"The details will follow tomorrow." This meant that, most likely, her fios would be revealed.

"Thanks, Mum—oh, and can you put on the third record of the Ring cycle?" Alice took her headphones and climbed back into bed. By this time the nasty dwarf Alberich had stolen the gold ring that the Rhine maidens guarded. Wotan, the one-eyed king of the gods, had now taken it from the dwarf, who then cursed the ring. *Always a curse,* Alice thought. Standard operating procedure in myths and fairy tales.

The gods were always flawed, but Wagner's Ring cycle was Hitler's favorite. He was said to play the records constantly and often staged parts of it in his various residences.

It had an almost gravitational pull on him—this mythic story of gods and giants, mystical mountains and caves, of dragons and Valkyries, the winged heroines who transported slain heroes to Valhalla.

But mostly the story was about power. Power and madness. No wonder Hitler loved it. Alice settled herself under the covers. Most people would not find this music soothing for sleep, but it was while she slept that her brain was, in one sense, most active. She had learned foreign languages this way, even retrieved the visual memory of the most intricate details of maps.

A ghostly face drifted through the fog of her dreams— *David, poor David. . . .* She shut off that part of her brain and let the rising crescendos of the Valkyrie battle cry fill her head.

Some said that if sung by the right soprano, the sound could peel the paint off walls. But Alice slept on in her own kind of peace as her brain whirred, absorbing every note and musical phrase. She smiled in her sleep as she felt a twinge in her back. *Am I sprouting wings?*

When she awoke in the morning, Alice had a deep inkling of her exact role in the mission. She was not an opera singer by any stretch of the imagination. But that wasn't the point. In the story, it was the Valkyrie Brünnhilde who brought down the gods and brought the slain heroes to Valhalla! She wouldn't have to be a soprano. Just clever. It all fit together now. The words she had read on the flight from England to Germany came back to her.

You are now officially part of Operation Valkyrie. OV is a plan first devised by the German Reserve Army to support Hitler, in case there was a general breakdown in civil order as a result of the possible Allied bombing of Berlin or an uprising of the millions of foreign forced laborers. . . . This plan has now been revised completely under the direction of Secret Germany, an anti-Nazi movement, to not only focus on a takeover, but on the assassination of Hitler. As you can see, the mission has been reversed. The target is now Hitler and the Nazis. Operation Valkyrie is a revolt.

But what the mission statement hadn't said was that *she* was the Valkyrie. She would not be the one to carry out the assassination of Hitler, but somehow she would move him toward his death. She would carry him to Valhalla on the wings of other Valkyries. In this sense she was to be his "winged servant." If he died, he was to be admitted to Valhalla, carried there on the wings of a Valkyrie. And she, Ute Schnaubel, was to become the substitute for the Valkyrie.

"Yoo-hoo! Ute! Darling, you have a visitor."

Alice, with the battle cry of the Valkyries still ringing in her head, got out of bed.

118

"Who, Mum?"

"A surprise. Wear your nice pinafore dress and the lovely eyelet-collar blouse."

"Ugh! That's so babyish." What was it with these German people and their little aprons?

"Believe me, this is hardly baby business." Her mother's eyes narrowed until they were fierce little slits of sparkling gray light. "Don't complain. This is important."

Who could this be? A surprise. Well, she could think of one person who would definitely be a surprise. Louise!

She quickly got herself dressed and came out with her hair neatly braided Brünnhilde style. All the Valkyries were usually shown with long blond braids. Her braids were not so long, nor so blonde.

She walked into the parlor of the garage apartment. The floor trembled slightly, as the parlor was directly over the car lift.

"Oh!" She gasped slightly. It was Colonel Stauffenberg. He stood erect, holding a lovely bunch of flowers—sunflowers! So she was right. He was her fios. The oak leaves of his handsome uniform seemed to glitter, as did his eye patch. He was her Wotan, from the opera! Of course, Wotan, king of the gods, who had given his eye to drink from the spring of knowledge. He was her fios as well as her case handler. Wotan must be his field name. In the myth and in the Ring cycle operas, Wotan was the god of war and the hero. And hadn't Stauffenberg been considered a warrior hero too? He had even lost his eye in this war. And now he was ready to turn on the evil leader, Adolf Hitler.

"Congratulations, Fräulein. A sunflower for a sunflower." He winked at her with his single eye. The effect was odd. It was as if his entire face went blank for a split second. Almost like that of a Rasa.

As she took the bouquet of flowers, she could feel that the paper they were wrapped in was sweet paper. She was excited. Maybe she would learn about where to put chalk marks or where to find dead drop locations. These were tricks she had mastered in Rasa camp. She had received the highest marks, plus fives, in all of these operations during war games the last week of camp. And when you won, you could be a spymaster during the games the following summer. It also meant that your bunk got double pudding at the final banquet. But darn it all, the real war had broken out by then. No camp. No double puddings. Pudding for the banquet was always Molly Morfitt's chocolate-and-raspberry triple layer cake squared. Which meant nine layers of the most delicious pudding ever created. Molly was Sir William's wife. Hence, the dining hall was called the Molly-Wills.

"And," Stauffenberg added, almost reading her mind, "the official certificate with the accompanying papers of instructions. Where to report and so forth."

"This is so kind of you. Will you excuse me while I put these lovely flowers in water?"

"Of course, and I must run off as well. Much to be done. I'm sure we shall see each other again."

"Yes, sir, I would enjoy that."

120

He nodded, then turned to her parents "Herr and Frau Schnaubel. It is always a pleasure."

As soon as the colonel had left, Posie Winfield turned to her daughter. "Your first!" She flashed a bright smile. "First bouquet, that is. You should go into the kitchen immediately and put them in water. There's a vase on the shelf by the sink."

Posie made sure to close the door behind her daughter as Alice reached for the vase and unwrapped the paper. She placed it on the counter and smoothed out the crinkles with her hand. The message was written in code one, as her legend had previously stated.

The principle subject is the Führer. His code name is Starling.

Alice's eyes opened wide. *Perfect,* she thought. Starlings were the most hated birds in Europe, and destructive to native wildlife. Large flocks could lay waste to fields of crops. They were also great transmitters of disease. She continued reading.

After the end of the school term, you will be installed in the Starling's Berlin household. This will bring you into the innermost domestic circle of the Führer, which includes his mistress, Eva Braun. She is easily impressed by the following: knowledge of movie stars, fashion, and silly romance novels. Make special note of these interests. Your duties will be to closely observe any changes in Starling's mental condition. We are anticipating an acute deterioration in his state of mind with the approach of the Allied invasion.

D-Day, the day that the Allied troops of British and American soldiers would land on the beaches in France, was the biggest secret in the world right now. Everyone knew it was coming, but the precise date and location were unknown. Most people were betting that the Allied forces would land near the Pas de Calais in northern France.

Alice continued reading.

Monitor Starling's condition with care, and report back when there are any signs of weakness. One indicator might be an increasing spasticity in his left arm—irregular or jerky movements. Another indicator would be a growing obsession with Wagner's Ring cycle.

You shall be contacted on or before June 15. As a member of the inner domestic circle of Starling's household, you will accompany the domestic staff to his retreats, the Wolfsschanze—Wolf's Lair—in East Prussia and the Berghof in the Bavarian Alps. Be prepared to bring a small valise with personal belongings. When and if you sense that Starling is on the brink of absolute collapse, you must signal your fios/handler, code name Wotan.

There it was, in black and white. Her fios and case handler were one and the same—Stauffenberg, the one-eyed colonel. Just like the one-eyed Wotan from the operas!

There was of course no name on the letter, but there was a faint sketch. Alice drew the paper closer to her eyes—it was the feather of a swan. Of course! The Valkyries had cloaks that were made of the plumage of swans. In the German and Norse myths, these creatures, the Valkyries, were winged young women who would swoop down across the battlefields and fly off with the most heroic soldiers killed in battle, carrying them to Valhalla. For this reason, they were called the choosers of the slain.

Like the first light of a breaking dawn it came to Alice. She was to document Hitler, in his growing madness, and report back to the British so that they would know when he was becoming weaker. Hitler did not want to die, but if he did, he wanted to be one of the chosen heroes taken to Valhalla. That was her mission, to document his every move and mood, identify his weaknesses, make him feel his destiny as one of the chosen.

Next, she found a list of her signal sites in Berlin, with the dead drop spots.

Kaiser Wilhelm Memorial Church, mailbox on the southeast corner of the Breitscheidplatz (shrub hedge at the back of the church's cemetery)

Traffic trash bin at the Palace Bridge, just in front of the Alte Kommandantur building (telephone booth at the corner, slide any message under the floor mat)

* *Lamppost near the Americano Café on Heide-strasse (fifty feet from the lamppost is a linden tree with a small hollow on the north side)*

* *Alley number seventeen trash bins behind the Americano Café (walking out of that alley there is another telephone booth—leave a message under the floor mat)*

* *Bench near the bear exhibit of the Berlin Zoo (twenty feet from that bench is a disused toolshed. Slip any message under the loose board on west side)*

* *Bench in the Tiergarten near the Folksong Memorial statue (empty fountain one hundred feet to the right of the bench. The rim of the fountain has several loose flat stones. On the north side there are three in a row. Pick any one of those three for a message)*

You will know your signal has been received if a thumbtack or a small piece of adhesive tape has been attached within inches of where you left the chalk mark. In case of a life-threatening emergency, to say "I am in danger," make the chalk mark, then proceed to the dead drop and leave something edible, like an apple, a small crust of bread, or a piece of candy.

FOURTEEN

"YOU-TAH BEACH"

For the next several days Alice had almost purposely avoided
going to the alley when she thought that David might be
there. How could she explain to David that she was really
working for the other side? It was of course tempting to tell
him. He might take heart, but it would be very dangerous.
And yet not telling him was equal to lying. It was, in fact,
living a lie. She had to face it—he was her only friend. Birgit, Margret, and Lena weren't really friends. They were, if
anything, tools through which she plied her trade—that of
being a spy. She fit in with them—with their school life, with
their gossip.

She had never really had had any friends except the Rasa
kids that she met at camp. And outside of Rasa camp, she
hadn't needed any friends because . . . because she had a sister. She clamped her eyes shut. She didn't want to think of

125

Louise. Think of her new face. Think of her perfume. But even worse was the fact that she could not be honest with David, and it pained her. Yes, she actually felt a sharpness someplace deep within her, like a small piece of glass cutting her.

She could not bear to think of him starving to death. So mostly she would go quite late at night and leave the food in a trash can. She could not risk coming back to see if he had retrieved it. She might say something—like the truth, she thought miserably. She might confess that she was a spy, and that would endanger them both. She just had to think positively, believe that he would find the food each time she left it.

June 15 loomed in her mind, as that was the day she would be accompanying the Führer to his Bavarian retreat. She knew her parents were dreading her departure. However, on June 5, she came to the breakfast table and found her parents with anything but dread on their faces. In fact, both their faces seemed bathed in a glow of happiness. "Any day now the invasion—any hour! The Allied troops will land." Alice dropped into a kitchen chair in disbelief. Her eyes opened wide.

"Truly?" she asked.

Her mother nodded. "I have no doubt." She sighed and then mused, "I wonder how our Louise is?" A silence fell on the family. Alan Winfield reached across and patted his wife's hand to quiet her. Posie got up and went to a cupboard where she had some of the sweet paper rolled up. She took a sheet and began to write out her message in code.

"I have no doubt that you will be called up early for your mission. So be prepared to start soon."

"I think I'll go for a run in the Tiergarten."

"Don't be long, dear," her mother said.

Alice purposely avoided the street, or rather the alley, of the whipped-cream house and cut to a less direct route to the park. She began to run down the bike trail toward the Lion's Gate bridge that crossed a wide stream. Splitting off from this trail, she headed toward the Blumenbeete, the flower beds that would be in their full glory this first week in June. She was sweating profusely by the time she stopped at a curved bed crammed with flowers in full bloom. *So beautiful,* she thought. *Almost as beautiful as English gardens.* Alice bent over to brace herself on her knees and take a few deep breaths. An explosion of pink and violet petunias appeared to be bickering for space.

"I'm the prettiest."

"No, I am. But look at those gaudy marigolds."

"Who would plant those garish showgirls by us?" another stately white delphinium seemed to sniff from its tall stalk.

But of course it was all in Alice's head. She loved to think of flowers conversing. They all had different personalities. She felt as if she could write a book or maybe a play—preferably a musical where all the actors would be flowers.

"Psst!" A hiss came from a dense hedge of yews just behind the delphiniums. "Ute!"

A face peeked through. *David? He recognizes me!* A wonderful feeling flooded through her. It had taken her classmates weeks upon weeks to remember her face, her name, anything except the fact that that she was the new student.

How had he recognized her? She was tempted to tell him to hide from the haughty delphinium.

She made her way toward the hedge and saw a squashed cluster of petunias, but they seemed to spring back up, and then she heard a kind of popping sound. Two white delphiniums crashed to the ground, their stems broken. *Die Invasion kommt,* she thought. *The invasion is coming.*

"You . . . you . . ." Alice was gasping. "You know me?"

"Of course, how could I not know you? I'm most likely alive because of you." A perplexed look crossed his face, casting it in a sad shadow. "And do you always talk to flowers?" A trace of a smile crossed his face, brightening his sallow complexion. "You did. Calling the marigolds garish showgirls. I couldn't quite make out the rest of your mutterings."

"I don't understand."

"Understand what?"

"That you recognized me."

She felt a panic begin to well up inside her. This was completely contrary to the second chapter of the L.F. guide, the *Leabhar Folachte*, old Gaelic for hidden book. It served as a kind of guide for the Rasa. The book no longer existed, but the lessons had been passed down from generation to generation since the sixteenth century. The book was said to have been the creation of William Morfitt and a Gaelic monk. It stated in the first chapter that outside of the familiar setting in which a non-Rasa might encounter her or his subject in the context of their mission, they would be unrecognizable. That state was often referred to as OC, short for out of context. Now David Bloom had just defied over five hundred years of Rasa history. He had recognized her!

"Are you saying you're not Ute?"

"Not exactly."

"You either are or you're not. But I say you are. I know you, Ute." Fear flooded her. How could he know her? Was this boy a double agent of some sort? She clasped David's hand. It was cold despite the warm weather. "Your hand's so cold."

"Are you trying to change the subject?" he snapped.

"No, no." She took a deep breath. "There is just so much I can't exactly explain right now." She leaned closer to him. "Look, David, I have to go away for a while. I won't be able to bring you food. But I'll try when I can."

"I was wondering why I never saw you in the alley lately. You must be coming when I'm inside the house, in the cellar."

"Yes, so your hiding place is still working?"

He nodded. "They drink a lot—the servants. Draining every wineglass that is left with anything in it at all. The butler often filches a whole bottle. Schmelling never notices. He's drunk half the time too. And his wife takes laudanum. You know what that is?"

Of course she knew the painkiller. It was prepared with

129

morphine and opium. But she didn't want to appear too knowledgeable. In Rasa camp chemistry labs, they had learned how to prepare it. It was sometimes essential for their work. Louise had told her that she learned more chemistry in Rasa camp than she ever learned in high school. She said that one of the hardest things for a Rasa kid was to disguise one's knowledge of chemistry.

Down the path from where Alice and David both crouched, they heard some voices rising in excitement.

"Nicht Pas de Calais!"

"Nein, Normandie. Utah Beach."

Both Alice and David froze as the voices approached. Then there were more voices, panicky voices and running feet.

"What is it?" David asked.

A smile broke across Alice's face. *Die Invasion kommt.* "Yes, they're talking about the invasion, but it's not where they expected it to be in France. Another part—it's Normandy instead."

"I don't understand."

"They were deceived by FUSAG."

"F-f-f-f . . . what?"

"FUSAG—the fictitious First US Army Group. Those Americans are very smart!"

"Where is . . . this place they're talking of? Ute Beach?"

Alice nearly laughed out loud. "No, not like my name, Ute. You-tah Beach."

FIFTEEN

WHILE HITLER SLEPT

Alice raced home after giving David a hug. All through the garden there were small clumps of people who talked in hushed voices, as if speaking out loud would somehow expedite the invasion. On street corners it was the same. They all knew it was coming, but they didn't know the real location: Normandy. According to the Germans, that was not where it was supposed to happen.

When Alice burst into the Bendlerstrasse garage, she found the mechanics standing about in stunned disbelief as a radio crackled reporting the invasion news. Walter, a top mechanic much favored by her father, turned around.

"Your papa is upstairs."

She paused a moment and looked at the car he was working on. It was Goebbels's Mercedes. She was sure. "He's not here," Walter replied. "Herr Goebbels is at the Berghof with the Führer."

"That's where the Führer is? Now?"

"Ja . . . enjoying the mountain air." If a voice could be said to have a smirk, Walter's did. Was he perhaps a double agent? No time to wonder. She rushed to the spiral staircase that led to the apartment.

Bursting in the door, she found her parents huddled by the wireless. Her father was turning the knobs to better tune the news. Both her parents looked up at her as she entered, their faces beaming. Alice slid into a chair.

"Kuschelwelpe hat geschlafen." The Cuddle Pup slept. Cuddle Pup was the Winfields' own code name for Hitler. They didn't know that for Alice the code name was different—Starling.

"Sleeping . . . I can't believe it."

"Believe it. Therefore, he could not be informed until . . ." Her father took out his pocket watch and looked at it. "Four hours ago. And the officer on duty has not yet authorized the closest of the German panzer tank divisions in Paris to advance. But thirteen thousand American paratroopers have dropped into Normandy since three a.m. Only the Cuddle Pup can launch the panzers."

Posie had a grin on her face. "He has to get up, brush his teeth, wash his face . . . move his bowels."

Alice made a face. She hated that expression. "He has to move his tanks, Mum, before his crap."

There was a knock on the door. The family quickly assumed doleful faces appropriate to the news. It was Walter, accompanied by a young officer who stepped into the room.

"I am here to escort Fräulein Ute Maria Schnaubel to her RP assignment. She is to pack a bag for herself, as she might be traveling to the Berghof. It is suggested that she bring warm clothes, as the weather is much chillier there. I shall wait outside while you prepare."

It did not take Alice long.

She soon came out of her room. Her parents suddenly looked pale and quite fragile as they stood by the door. The time had come. Her very first mission.

"Try not to cry, Mum, Dad. I'll be fine. And he said I might not leave right away."

"Yes, of course, dear," Posie replied, but her lower lip was trembling.

"You are prepared!" Her father's voice was low and guttural. His eyes were suddenly suffused with a steely glow—a glow of belief, it seemed to Alice.

Two minutes later she was in the back of a Volkswagen with her bag, and the young fellow was driving.

"This is an odd route to get to the chancellery on Wilhelmstrasse," she commented.

"We are not going directly to the chancellery."

"Oh, I thought that was where my RP was."

"Not exactly."

"Where exactly are we going?"

"The Führerbunker."

"The Führerbunker!"

"Yes, it is virtually next door, but we only approach by this route. It's the quickest way into the complex."

Alice knew about this complex. It was no secret. It had been built during the renovation of the Old Chancellery, maybe four or five years before, when the war began. It was located beneath the garden of the Old Reich Chancellery. It was essentially an air-raid shelter with an underground web of tunnels and rooms. But the word "bunker" wasn't quite right, as it was rumored to be very lavishly decorated. There were chandeliers, and an extensive wine cellar with many bottles of the finest champagne.

They now turned through an entry gate, and the Volkswagen pulled up to a parking space in a courtyard in front of a stubby peaked roof tower—the guardhouse, presumably. A man came out.

"We are expected," the driver said. The guard nodded.

"Park over there, sir."

They pulled into a small parking lot. Getting out of the car, Alice followed the driver, who carried her bag across a small expanse of paving stones. In a wall of dressed stones, a small wood-paneled door opened. *Obviously the servants' entrance,* Alice thought. An elderly lady with a crinkled-up face as wizened as a dried apple walked toward them. Alice nearly gasped out loud. She was the quintessential roly-poly old lady from a book of fairy tales. This woman, with her headscarf tied babushka style, her apron, and her voluminous skirt, looked like the old woman who lived in a shoe, with her numerous children spilling out of it every which way.

"This way, dearie," the woman said. "I am Gudrun. Frau Gudrun Weissmann, and I'll show you to your quarters and then explain your tasks here."

"Yes, Frau Weissmann." The air was dank and suffused with a tinge of mold.

"Good girl, I can tell you are obedient. Follow me."

Frau Weissmann had a figure that reminded Alice of two blobs of dough piled on top of each other. Alice thought of the snow-people cookies that she and Louise would make for Christmas, three-dimensional cookies that they would decorate with chocolate frosting hats and buttons made of red hots candies, with raisins for eyes. She shut her eyes tight, remembering again the wafting scent of the Laurel Bright perfume that Louise wore. How could her nose cling to something so ephemeral? It really wasn't the fragrance she clung to but their fight. The argument. The words like darts that they had hurled at each other.

"Now, dearie." Gudrun turned her head. "When we go around the next bend, don't look to the right. Try to cover that side of your face with your hand."

"Why?"

"Art, degenerate art!"

"Then why do you have it here?"

Frau Gudrun Weissmann stopped abruptly. Her little eyes like raisins and appeared to grow darker.

"After this war is over and we are victorious, we shall sell it and build a beautiful museum to honor our Führer."

But Alice did slide her eyes to the right. There was a luminous pastel of a woman in a prim blue blouse. She was certain it must be a Degas. Hardly degenerate. Not a bit of flesh showing. And next to it was what appeared to be an Italian Renaissance painting. Maybe a Caravaggio. Alice had seen a few Caravaggios in the National Gallery of Art in London when they had lived there.

"No peeking now!" The frau's voice rang out. But Alice did peek, and then stopped cold as she saw a powerful radiance glowing a few yards ahead. *Klimt!* She knew about this painting, a portrait of a wealthy Jewish lady from Vienna. It had been commissioned by her husband and confiscated by the Nazis when they marched into Austria. Now here it was, moldering away in the dampness, countless meters underground in the lair of this mad man.

Frau Weissmann turned down another path. "Follow me!" she called out gaily. "The next door on the right is where you shall be staying. The room is tiny but comfortable."

Alice stepped into the space. It was not simply tiny but minuscule. The bed took up three quarters of the room.

"Extra blankets under the bed. Washroom is down the hall. A shelf for your books—I know you are a very good student. So you must have books. Is that what's in your backpack?"

"A couple, but mostly clothes."

"I believe that you'll be wearing a uniform."

"Uniform?" Alice's heart sank. A gray uniform like the SS. Or would it be the drab greenish-gray of the army or the blue-gray of the Luftwaffe, the air army? "What kind of uniform?"

"Oh, just a domestic one—a black dress with a nice crisp white apron, as I imagine you'll help serve tea and such." *And such . . . ? Just what was "and such"?*

"Now put your backpack down, and I'll take you down the hall to the domestic quarters of the Führer." They walked on a bit more. There were double doors made of steel ahead. "Through these doors." She took out a key and unlocked a door. "This is the honorable Fräulein Braun's bedroom, or boudoir, as she prefers to call it."

Of course, thought Alice. The expression "honorable Fräulein," Alice would soon learn, was the form of address that all people of the household would use when speaking about Eva Braun, the Führer's mistress. The words should be considered a sign of respect or politeness. But Alice would soon realize that people, particularly when the Führer was not present, tended to put their own twists on the phrase. It was almost as if a smirk was embedded in the very words . . . perhaps a note of derision that hinted that Fräulein Braun did not yet have the right to be called Frau Hitler, since they had never married.

* * *

Although the rest of the world did not know much about Eva Braun, the sweet paper had offered Alice some insight into this shallow and rather silly woman. From a sweet paper Alice had learned that Eva Braun was obsessed with movie stars, fashion, and European socialites. The words "feather-brained" and "inconsequential" were used in the description. Nevertheless, she was Hitler's girlfriend.

Frau Weissmann opened the door. Even if it had not been in the bunker, it was a ridiculous room. Alice felt as though she had walked into a massive cloud of cotton candy—or fairy floss, as it was sometimes called. Everything was pink and puffy. There was a couch that was upholstered in an elaborate floral brocade. A gilt-edged writing desk that matched a coffee table with an elegant tea service set upon it. The wallpaper appeared to be embossed with a fussy design of pink and silver flowering vines scrambling over a deeper pink background.

In the middle of the room stood an open and empty steamer trunk. "Now," Frau Weissmann pointed to the empty trunk. "I have a list here, prepared by Liesl, of the things that Fräulein Braun requires to be packed up and sent to the Berghof."

"And who is Liesl, might I ask?"

"Oh, Fräulein Braun's personal maid. Liesl Ostertag. Here is a list of the dresses. If you have any questions, just come and ask me. But Frau Ostertag has given a very detailed description of each gown, so you shouldn't have trouble finding them." She took a deep breath, and her ample breasts seemed to heave under the bodice of the apron. "However, there is something of a more delicate nature I must ask of you."

Oh God, Alice thought. *Is this going to be something about Eva Braun packing sanitary napkins?*

"You know how our Führer is displeased with makeup, cosmetics, and such. He feels that they use animal products—pig grease or something. But Fräulein Braun does like makeup. Very light makeup. So, there are rules at the Berghof—no red lipstick, no nail polish. Fräulein Braun gets her makeup specially made for her by the chemist shop just a few blocks away—a very light powder and rouge, the palest pink lipstick and clear nail polish. There is a separate list of these items, all which can be picked up within a ten-minute walk from here. You won't have to pay. Fräulein Braun has a charge there. When you finish packing, you can set off for those items." Frau Weissmann took a deep breath. "Now can you prepare this by tomorrow morning?"

"Yes, I believe so."

"Good, we shall be sending the trunk ahead."

"Ahead of what?"

"Ahead of you, my dear."

"Am I going to the Berghof?"

"Absolutely. You will love it. Fresh mountain air, hiking, helping with the clothes—the parties. And oh yes, there are to be scenes performed from the Ring cycle. It will be delightful. Lots of music. Oh my, our Führer loves his entertainment and operas."

Delightful? The Germans were losing on the Russian front. The Allied armies of Americans and British had just landed in France with over 150,000 troops. The invasion had come. And what were the leaders of Germany doing? Listening to music!

SIXTEEN

A FACE IN A CROWD

"It's not forever, Mum. Think of it as camp."

"Hruumph." Her father gave a low growl.

But she was excited to begin her mission. Everything until now in her life had been preparation—preparation for anything that might occur, no matter what the mission. She had learned how to jump from aircraft. She had a limited knowledge of aviation—she knew how to take off and land. And she was familiar with dozens of codes, not to mention all the languages she had learned. She regretted that there had not been time for one last visit to David. She just wished he could find more food, although she had brought him a fair amount. She hoped he could make it last. At least it had been getting warmer for several days now. Survival should be easier.

The following morning, she had accomplished all the

errands that Gudrun had sent her on. There was time for her to return to the apartment over the garage for the night, but she was supposed to be back at the Führerbunker by nine o'clock sharp.

The same young man came to pick her up in the same Volkswagen. Frau Weissmann was waiting for her as they drove up. She appeared slightly agitated. The two blobs of dough seemed to be rising.

Then she gasped. "Where's the girl?" she asked.

"Right here, Frau Weissmann."

"Oh, forgive me, child. I didn't recognize you. For some reason."

"Oh, it's me," Alice said quickly. "Ute Schnaubel. Maybe it's my hair?" Alice had learned that it was always good to give people a reasonable excuse as to why they might not remember her. "I had it in a half Gretchen, you know. Back down, and then a single pigtail wrapped across the back."

"Ah yes, of course. The half Gretchen is more sophisticated, makes you look a bit older."

"Yes, that's what my mother says." *Total lie!*

"But thank heavens you're here. A message just came through. Fräulein Braun needs the new movie magazines. They just came out this morning. The newsstand on the corner of Anhalterstrasse and Wilhelmstrasse will have them."

"Do I need money?"

"No, we have a charge there too. They are expecting you. Now run along, dear, your driver will be here soon."

142

I have a driver! For some reason this surprised her. She had thought she would be going on the train.

There was a throng of people at the newsstand because everyone wanted to read about the invasion. Men in tan uniforms with elaborate patches on their collars elbowed their way through the crowds. The SA, Hitler's paramilitary, a private army of sorts that had distinguished themselves with their wanton violence was shouldering their way through the crowds. People instantly backed off to let them through.

"Out . . . out!" The news vendor shouted. "*Völkischer Beobachter* out since an hour ago. *Vossischer Zeitung* out from five minutes ago, along with *Das Reich*. Read all about the invasion here!"

"Propaganda shit," she heard someone mutter behind her, but when she turned to look, she could only see the back of someone hurriedly walking away. The other people were pressing forward. Alice wormed her way toward the vendor. "I'm here for Frau Gudrun Weissmann."

"Ah yes! I have the order." He turned away, ducked under the counter, and came up with a net bag. "I couldn't get the latest of *Style Now*, but I do have *Modenschau*, *Fashion Show*, and guess who's on the cover?"

"Wouldn't know," Alice answered.

"Duchess of Windsor. Once we win the war, she'll be a queen in England, and her husband the duke will be back on his rightful throne as king!"

Dream on, Alice thought. The Duke and Duchess of

Windsor were Nazi sympathizers, and although they were royal, Prime Minister Churchill had essentially kicked them out of England and given them some dumb post far away in the Caribbean, where the duke became governor of the Bahamas. Stalwart Princess Elizabeth would become queen. She was eighteen years old and next in line. Some said the duke and duchess would never be allowed to set foot in England again.

"Fräulein Braun loves the duchess," the news vendor said.

Fräulein Braun is an idiot, thought Alice. But she smiled sweetly and replied, "Of course, Fräulein Braun is a woman of great taste and style."

"You said it, sister!" He smiled warmly at her. She noticed that his left eye was peculiar. It seemed frozen. *Of course.* A glass eye. A casualty of the Great War, World War I. More than a fifth of the returning soldiers from that war had lost some body part—arms, legs, and there were horrific eye injuries. This fellow obviously could not afford one of the expensive false eyes that were sold in the more elegant parts of the city. There had actually been a shortage of the kind of glass necessary for those. So this was a ceramic eye, perhaps, glazed and painted. It was very disorienting, for it did not reflect light. It had none of the focusing characteristics of a real eye or a glass eye.

"Sister," he had said to her merrily. The word was still ringing in her head when something very peculiar occurred. There was a crowd of people streaming by her, and one face seemed to float out. She blinked. The word "sister" was still reverberating in her head. But that face! She turned around to catch another glimpse, but the girl was gone—that face in that crowd could have been Louise. Was it Louise? How could it have been?

She blinked now and craned her neck. The crowd ebbed around her. Where was that face? She felt as if she was a rock in the middle of a fast-moving stream and hundreds of faces were eddying around her like flowing water. Was it a singular face in a crowd or a crowd in one face? Was it her sister's new face or was it the old face—but here in Berlin? Impossible. What strange refractions in her own eye had caused this? Were the refractions in her eye or in her mind? Was her mind splintering her thoughts like a prism splintered color?

Acute angles of memory, desire and loss were colliding. She had to put this out of her mind. She must not be distracted. She had a mission. Operation Valkyrie. She had committed to memory the messages on the sweet paper she had received from Wotan, her fios—Colonel Claus von Stauffenberg. She was a part of Operation Valkyrie now. She could not afford to be distracted.

Fifteen minutes later Alice climbed into the back seat of an official SS automobile, a gleaming Mercedes-Benz. On the latest cover of *Filmwelt*, *Movie World*, the haunting eyes of Hildegard Knef peered out. Hildegard was a newly discovered actress but destined to become a star—or so said Birgit from school. Alice had bumped into Birgit just yesterday when she had gone to pick up the cosmetics. But Birgit hadn't even remembered who she was. Two days she had missed school, and now the memory of her had been completely erased from every atom in Birgit's brain. She of course was very apologetic when Alice reminded her. "Oh, of course! Ute. And when do you begin your RP?"

"Well, now. Actually."

"Where?"

"Uh . . ." She decided not to say the Führerbunker. "At the Reich Chancellery, the residential quarters."

And now today she was riding in the back seat of this luxury automobile. The driver's name was Hans. She saw him glancing back at her through his rearview mirror frequently. It gave her the creeps. She dipped her head and kept looking at the magazines.

She opened a fashion magazine. The one with the Duchess of Windsor on the cover. The duchess was as thin as a knitting needle and wearing an evening gown that poured over her like cream. Around her neck was a choker of emeralds and diamonds, on her head a tiara. *No, that does not work,* Alice thought. *The necklace is too heavy for that dainty little tiara. It doesn't balance.* It made her look quite silly.

They were clear of the traffic out of Berlin in less than a half an hour and speeding along the newly completed autobahn toward the town of Berchtesgaden in the Bavarian Alps, the southeast corner of Germany. It was this highway

146

that allowed Hitler to so easily invade Poland and take it over. What would happen now? Alice wondered. That highway that allowed the Nazis to go right into Poland might be a two-way street. Would it give the Russians, who were on England's side and France's side and the Americans' side, a clear path for them to swarm into Berlin and take the city? Wouldn't that help to win the war? If the Russians came in from the east and the Americans and the English came from the west, they could pinch the Nazis—pinch them to defeat, to death. But Alice knew she was getting ahead of herself. The Americans had only landed on those beaches in France a few days before.

Because Alice was in an official government vehicle, they could travel at a very high speed. The speedometer was registering one hundred and thirty kilometers per hour, at least thirty-two kilometers per hour faster than regular cars. Her own head began to hang heavy as if in fact she was supporting a massive crown and not some teensy tiara. Her lids drooped. She felt the magazine slip off her lap to the floor. But she did not bother to pick it up. Then, less than a minute later, she jerked awake.

That face again. It couldn't have been Louise. Her sister was back in England. She was working at Bletchley. They had received that deeply coded message weeks ago. There was no way she could be in Berlin. And yet there was something about that face.

She replayed the moments in her head. She softly bit her lip in concentration. Had she smelled the scent? Was there any Laurel Bright perfume in the air? The only odor she could recall was the smell of a burning cigar jammed in the mouth of someone rushing by.

Then a moment within those moments came back to her. It was just before she had turned around. She and that young woman had locked eyes. Alice had gasped, and yet her sister betrayed no sign of recognition. It was as if Louise's eyes were artificial—ceramic like the news vendor's, that neither reflected or refracted.

A sort of nausea swept over her. She prayed she wouldn't be carsick. She clamped her eyes shut. The driver must have glanced at her in the rearview mirror.

"You okay, Fräulein?"

"Uh . . . yes, a bit queasy maybe."

"Ach! You and my wife. There's a rest area coming up soon. Very excellent facilities."

"Yes, that would be nice," Alice replied.

Within ten minutes they were at the rest area. Alice made her way to the toilet and went through the door labeled Damen. She went up to the sink and splashed cold water on her face. She immediately felt better. After going into a stall, then washing her hands again, she went back to the Mercedes, where her driver was lounging against the front fender smoking.

"Feel better?"

"Yes, yes, I do. Thank you."

"You can almost see the Kehlsteinhaus from here. That's almost two hours from here. So that means we'll be at the Berghof within the hour. Not much longer."

The Kehlsteinhaus she thought, *the Eagle's Nest*. She had heard about it. It was higher up, on the summit of a rocky outcrop. There the highest German officers met with their Führer, where that demonical predator, beaked and taloned, ready for prey, occasionally roosted while planning his exterminations of millions. But he was soon to be prey himself. Alice was unsure of when or how, but she knew she must be ready. There would be a contact to whom she could deliver her observations on the mental state of the Führer and any changes in his schedule.

She also knew that she would be seeing Stauffenberg himself. A sweet paper had come through hours before her departure, saying that he would be going to the Berghof to discuss the Valkyrie plan—the original one, of course, to prepare for a possible breakdown in civil order that might follow an Allied bombing. Wotan was the perfect officer to update the Führer, as he was soon to be promoted to the position of full colonel and chief of staff to the commander of the German army.

They left the autobahn and continued on a narrower road at a much slower speed.

"Over there!" The driver pointed. The shadow of a mountain loomed up against the sky. "Watzmann," he said. "Third highest mountain in Germany."

"Aaah!" Alice made what she felt was an appropriate response.

"Three peaks—Mittelspitze, Südsptize, but I'm afraid you can't see Hocheck from here. Bit foggy on top. But the weather is going to clear soon."

Then they were gliding down into a valley and began winding through a wooded area.

"River Berchtesgadener Ache," the driver announced as he drove onto a bridge. There was soon another sign for the Hotel Platterhof. "Bigwigs stay there." The driver pointed to a half-timbered building. Each window had a flower box spilling with pink and blue blossoms.

"But the biggest of the bigwigs have homes," the driver said, pointing to the left. "Albert Speer. His villa. You know, the Führer's favorite architect." The driver took one hand off the wheel. "The whole lot, Fräulein. You are at the center of it all. I mean, of course there's Berlin and the chancellery, but right here in the mountains is true center. Everyone comes here." He paused a moment, then pointed ahead to the right.

He'd suddenly become very talkative. "And guess whose house that is at the top?"

"No idea," Alice answered. He clearly enjoyed educating her.

"Reichsmarschall Hermann Göring."

"He's head of the air force," Alice replied.

"Ever seen him in person?"

"Only photos."

"He's definitely a fat fellow. And just below Göring's house is Martin Bormann's villa. Head of the Nazi party. Has ten kids! Yes, ten! Göring, just one." He now emitted a harsh laugh. Then he paused in this voluble account. "And now you, little one."

"Yes . . . me?"

"So what's the story?"

"What do you mean?"

"Why are you here? Are you a cousin or a friend of Fräulein Braun?"

"Oh no. Never met her. I'm just a Reich Praktikum kid."

"Aaaah! You must be very smart. Well, they'll find something very smart for you to do, I'm sure."

Yes, she wanted to say, *like assassinate Hitler.* Although she knew that she would not be the one to pull the trigger or set off the bomb. She was unsure of the details of the assassination. She was there to provide information. And she was ready.

They had by this time passed through two checkpoints. The driver slowed down, and as soon as he stuck his head out, they waved him through. *Lousy security,* Alice thought. How did they know that she wasn't in the back seat with a gun cleverly covered but pressed up against the driver's seat? Or with a bomb that could be detonated?

They had just driven through a stone archway and begun to climb a steep hill.

"Now if you're so smart . . . ," the driver began slowly. Where was this going? Alice wondered.

"Yes?"

"I told you Reich Minister Bormann has ten children."

"Yes, you said that."

"But how did Hermann Göring, who is very very fat, who weighs three hundred and fifty pounds, how did he even manage to have a child? It's a mystery. Poor woman."

A quiet terror spread through Alice. Men who spoke like this to girls her age were dangerous. This was his first step. She was trapped in this car. He looked in the rearview mirror. She watched his thick lips spread into a salacious smile. What should she do? What could she say? Could she pretend to throw up? Or could she lie? Tell him that she was a niece of Minister Goebbels and would report back on the driver's behavior? But then that might make her more memorable. That was the last thing she wanted to do. An idea came into her head.

This was where all her summer camp acting lessons came into play. She must remain calm, even thought her heart was pounding as hard as the thudding of this diesel engine. She leaned forward and locked her eyes on his in the mirror. His hand lay casually on the back of the seat. She wanted to clamp her teeth on it as hard as possible and bite his fingers through to the bone. But she didn't.

"Herr Chauffeur, you touch one hair on my head, and I report you to the secret police. Do you know what the punishment is for sexually molesting an RP girl?" She paused a fraction of a second. "Castration." He turned pale and put his hand back on the wheel. There was of course no such punishment.

In another two minutes they were pulling up to the villa of the Berghof. "Now, when I get out of this car, I shall forget what you told me, and you can forget you ever saw me." *It will be easy,* she thought.

SEVENTEEN

A RHINE MAIDEN

"*Achtung! Rheintöchter!* Yes, attention, Rhine maidens!"
Winifred Wagner, the director of this performance from
the Ring cycle, was charging around on the stage in her
semi-dirndlish dress. A full-blown dirndl with puff sleeves
and white apron would not have suited Frau Wagner. The
daughter-in-law of Richard Wagner, Winifred was a large
woman who could have been a Valkyrie herself.

"Now let me explain. What we are doing here is not, of
course, a full opera, but scenes. You do not have to sing, but
you present a motionless scene as music plays on the gramophone. I arrange all of you in a pose as the curtain opens. I
stand at the conductor's podium, and you watch my baton.
When it moves, you change your pose." She delivered these
instructions as crisply as any drill sergeant in the Führer's

154

army. "You remain silent as the singers on the record do all the singing. But it helps if you keep your mouths open . . . like this . . ." She then drew her rather thin lips into an oval shape. Alice noticed that Frau Wagner had very bad teeth.

"There are only four different poses within the scene we are staging tonight. In the first pose, you are sitting on the rocks of the river, guarding the treasure of the Rhinegold, as the dwarf Alberich has just appeared. He is dazzled by your beauty. But most of all Alberich wants the treasure. This is an opera all about the gods, their ruler, and the quest for power. Whoever gets the ring possesses power. All about questing for power, and then the collapse of everything—the Götterdämmerung, the Twilight of the Gods. That's it, in a nutshell."

Alice learned that every summer, excerpts from Hitler's favorite opera were performed here, in a series of these tableaux vivants. A stage was erected. Old costumes brought out of storage. And since the entire orchestra could not be transported, the records played on a gramophone.

Alice had been drafted into the performance almost as soon as she had arrived. They were now rehearsing. She was one of the Rhine maidens.

"Now which one are you?" Frau Wagner demanded. "Woglinde?"

"No, I'm to be Flosshilde," Alice replied.

"I'm Woglinde." A tall and frail-looking girl stepped forward.

"Aah yes, Herta."

"And I'm Wellgunde," said another.

Frau Wagner nodded. "Of course, and the new girl here is Flosshilde." She paused briefly. "And what's your name again?"

"Ute . . . Ute Schnaubel."

"Right, right. Not sure why I can't remember that. Your face is lovely. Reminds me of Gerte Wertheimer, who sang the role of Sieglinde in the 1929 performance. She brought down the house!"

My intentions exactly, Alice thought.

"Now you go to stage left and sit on that rock. And you, Woglinde, sit at her feet, and Wellgunde, you go to the right of . . . uh . . . pardon me, Flosshilde." She paused. "What's your real name again?"

"Ute."

"Good. Now when the music begins again, you, Floss-hilde, raise your hands—as a teacher might. One finger pointing as if to remind them, not scold them, of their sacred duty to guard the gold at the bottom of the river. You understand, Flosshilde?"

"Yes, Frau Wagner."

"Perfect. Now try it with the music playing. Cue the music, please," she said.

A lovely female voice sang out, and Alice opened her mouth slightly as if singing. "Guard the gold! Father warned us of such a foe!"

Alice soon caught a glimpse of Eva Braun, Hitler's girl-friend, sulking in a corner of the Berghof theater. Eva Braun was pretty, not beautiful—but Alice realized she had honed the skill of sulking to an art form. A talent that was only equaled by her abilities with a curling iron. Gossip had it that Frau Wagner asked her to help with the Rhine maidens' hair, which was supposed to flow over their shoulders like the curling waters of the Rhine.

The performance would be this evening. Alice had not yet even glimpsed the Führer. But he was expected to attend. So her first view of him might be from the stage. She had settled into her quarters. There was a small narrow window, like the ones in English medieval castles called arrow-slot win-dows. When she was not performing on the stage, she had been informed by the head housekeeper, Elisabeth Kalham-mer, that she would be serving in the dining room and at tea. No one was ever to address the Führer without first being addressed by him. Not even to offer a cup of tea.

"He's not a talkative man," Frau Kalhammer emphasized. "He does not like idle conversation." Alice was informed that his favorite food was a special apple cake baked by the chef. It was referred to as Führer cake. He ate it at all times of the day and night. He even walked down to the kitchens in the middle of the night to have a slice. If perchance one was on late-night kitchen duty, there was no need to ask what he wanted, but to just cut him a slice of the cake and pour a glass of apple juice to accompany it.

Alice immediately made a mental note of this. She must offer to be on night duty in the kitchen. When better to observe him, assess his state? But most importantly, she must do what was called by the Rasa a reverse projection profile analysis, or RPPA. In short, whose image would the Führer possibly be capable of projecting on to her face? What might emerge out of the blankness of her face that could inspire him, excite him, or make him cower in the dark corners of the shredded sleep of a nightmare?

It was rather close to WTS, the wishful thinking syndrome that had made Louise seem like the movie star Rita Hayworth to the flirtatious young man that time in the pub who'd just seen her latest movie. He had projected an image that played in his mind, and essentially had sketched that image on Louise's blank face. In that way, Alice, or rather Ute Schnaubel, could haunt Hitler's dreams. It was a mental process as mysterious in a way as reading tea leaves or tarot cards.

Since the invasion on the beaches of Normandy, the Allied troops had met with more success. The Americans and the British were on track to take the French port of Cherbourg. Rome had fallen to the Allies the day before D-Day. On the eastern front, the Russian Red Army's offensive against so-called neutral Finland was succeeding. And yet, here at the Berghof, the merry lederhosen folk were fiddling with operas as the jaws of war were clamping down in a death grip on Germany.

She recalled last year at summer camp, sitting with a small group of other Rasa kids in a dark room as JoJo McPhee, a veteran Rasa agent, led a workshop on reverse projection profile analysis. On the movie screen was the photograph of one Alfred Stegall, a Rasa during the first World War. "This is Agent Stegall. He successfully defused a line of sapper explosives that were set to go off in Belgium; they would have killed five hundred British soldiers who were part of a key line of defense. The explosives never did go off, and thus a significant battle was won." JoJo McPhee had paused to let that sink in. "Now, campers, I want you to look at Alfred Stegall's face and give me your first impressions."

One hand went up. "Nice-looking bloke," said Hildy, who had been a tentmate of Alice's.

"Well groomed," said another.

"Indeed!" replied JoJo. "No beard or mustache. He followed the fellow for several hours in the town. Saw who and where he went, what he liked. The sapper had attended a movie that featured his favorite actress, Lillian Schon, a star of early silent movies. Alfred had found out that the man had attended this movie at least three times." The counselor flashed a picture on the screen. "This is Lillian Schon in her movie *The Haunting of Margaret*, where she played a lost but beautiful young girl in a haunted forest, a fantasy film."

The photograph showed a young woman with very dark hair and a gauzy black headscarf tied back bandanna style. The counselor then clicked the projector again and two faces appeared—Alfred Stegall's, with a black rag on his head, and next to it the original picture she had shown of the clean-shaven man.

"Now you can see for yourself, Alfred bears no resemblance to the beautiful Lillian Schon. But with this scarf and a certain tip of his head, he succeeded in evoking the image of her in the mind of the enemy, the sapper. He followed the sapper to the movie theater twice to see the film. The sapper was ripe. The beautiful actress's image had been impressed on the sapper's mind somewhat like the image that lingers on one's retina after a person stares at a bright object. Rarely has a Rasa of a different gender accomplished drawing out an afterimage of the opposite gender. I think there have been only three recorded times in the history of the Rasas! But when Alfred appeared in the tunnel where the sapper was laying the fuse, the man was rendered helpless.

"He made no move against Alfred, who merely asked him to wait for a moment around the next bend. Alfred cut the cable and left. The sapper was waiting for who knows how long before he came out of this fog of confusion. This is wishful thinking syndrome. Buried deep in the sapper's conscience was the image of the actress. By wearing the scarf, Alfred had manipulated the sapper's mind until the movie star image came to the surface and he projected it onto Alfred's face. We call this not simply wishful thinking syndrome but reverse projection phenomena."

"Did Alfred promise to kiss the fellow?" one kid asked.

"Ooooh!" The campers squirmed.

"Who knows? Maybe. The point is, the job was done. Five hundred lives were saved." JoJo looked at each Rasa in the small group intently. "This talent that we have, children, although few could match Alfred's, has to do with the disturbance of neural pathways and certain receptors in the brains of our quarry, the enemy, that we are capable of altering because of the anonymity of our own faces as Rasas. It is, oddly enough, a gift. Rasa seldom require weapons. We can destroy, create havoc, in mostly nonviolent ways."

Alice's first glimpse of the Führer was when she stepped up to take her bow at the end of the performance. He leaped up from his seat and clapped ferociously. His mouth stretched open, making a dark black hole. The little toothbrush mustache danced up and down above his mouth. There appeared to be something slightly wrong with his left arm. Alice detected some spastic movements, and sometimes his hands could not meet together in clapping. She was so distracted by this she did not notice at first that at the far end of the first row, where the Führer sat, was Wotan! Yes, Colonel Stauffenberg. The colonel was now walking up to the stage with what appeared to be several bouquets of flowers. Mounting the steps, he nodded at the Rhine maidens. He turned toward the audience, which now quieted.

"It is my honor to present each of the lovely young Rhine maidens with a bouquet of flowers in honor of the lovely performance they gave tonight." He walked toward Elke, one of the serving girls, the one whose hair she had heard backstage had been singed by Eva Braun. Then he came Irmgard Bormann, one of Martin Bormann's ten children, who was perhaps a year younger than Alice.

Then finally he came to Alice. He smiled tightly, a ghost of a smile really. He seemed exceptionally tense. His single blue eye appeared almost as dark as the eye patch covering his missing eye. How could an eye as blue as a cloudless sky look so dark? But as soon as she grasped the bouquet, she realized that the stems of the flowers were wrapped in sweet paper.

She went directly to her bedroom following the performance. There would be more rehearsals tomorrow for other scenes from the opera that were planned over the course of the next few days. After locking the door, she sat on her bed and unwrapped the stems of the daisies and asters. Smoothing out the paper, she read the first sentence—which was total nonsense, but established the code that the message was written in. Only Rasa codes were used, and they had nothing to do with any of the ciphers used by any of the Allies. This code was written in R-cipher eighty-eight. The same code that had been used by Rasas serving Queen Elizabeth during the war with Spain and the defeat of the Spanish Armada.

It was a great code. It had never been broken, not since the

Armada. It was indecipherable to even the most skilled code breakers. There were not simply dots and dashes or inversions of words or nonsense rhymes. No, this code was done with inverted Gaelic script, an "insular script," a medieval form of writing, that was used by Irish monks in the sixteenth century.

When Alice smoothed the sweet paper and saw the R-cipher eighty-eight, she felt a slight pang. It was Louise who had drilled her relentlessly on this code, three years before. Her sister had won the highest prize in cryptology and, as Louise had put it, her little sister could not let the family down. She must do as well if not exceed Louise's own score. As it turned out, Alice had tied with her sister, receiving the highest score possible of one thousand in both decoding and encrypting. She read the rather short note immediately. Speed, of course, was of the essence.

Your contact will appear within a very few days. You will recognize her immediately, even though you have never seen her before. Her name is Hedwig. She is about nine years old.

Nine years old! *Good heavens,* Alice thought.

Any observations you have of Starling—his decline in health, mental state, any talk you overhear—report verbally to Hedwig. She is very young, but fierce. She

lives with her parents, long-experienced field agents
on a small farm. This will be a kind of brush contact
but slightly prolonged. She often swims at the lake.

Hedwig will function not only as a receptor but also
as a transmitter.

Interesting! A kind of brush contact but slightly prolonged? She was not sure what that meant, exactly. So this little nine-year-old girl would not only receive Alice's updates on the condition of the Führer, but also report to Alice vital information that she received.

There was a rough map sketched on the paper that showed the directions to the farm from the Berghof. It was no more than a fifteen-minute walk, not far from a lake called Königssee, a favorite swimming spot for tourists. This entire region of the Obersalzburg must be thick with spies, and not just Rasas like her. Who else might be one? Might there be someone, aside from herself, right here in the Berghof?

Alice sat quietly on her bed for several minutes, tearing the sweet paper into strips, slipping them into her mouth and letting them dissolve on her tongue. She closed her eyes. She remembered Louise drilling her on this code so vividly. Surely Louise must still be at Bletchley in England, deciphering codes. The girl she had glimpsed in Berlin could not have possibly been her.

It struck Alice suddenly that perhaps she herself was falling victim to WTS, wishful thinking syndrome, as she longed for her sister, Louise. Louise with her old face, not the new one. But it simply made no sense whatsoever that Louise could be in Berlin. She had quit. She had undergone hours of surgery so she could leave.

EIGHTEEN

THE CHOOSER OF THE SLAIN

The sunshine was brilliant on the terrace as Alice, now dressed in a pink dirndl with a blue bodice and puffy sleeves, walked among the guests with a tray of lemonade. The dark evening service uniform was apparently disregarded for afternoon tea parties. There were platters of pastries set out on round tables. Hitler himself, with his dog, Blondi, a mottled gray-and-black German shepherd on a short leash, strode about the terrace. Eva Braun's dogs, two Scottish terriers, Stasi and Negus, enjoyed somewhat longer leashes, until one peed on a waiter's trouser cuff and was instantly yanked away by another waiter. Eva looked at him furiously, as if to say, "How dare you? Don't you know who I am?" But she merely pressed her mouth shut and stared down at the stone terrace.

Of course they all knew who she was. The Führer's mistress—not a wife. She was the honorable Fräulein Braun, gracious—which they said scornfully behind her back. Honorable seemed to Alice a very affected term. But in this case it was used sarcastically, which gave more than a whiff of what people really thought about Eva Braun. The very use seemed cruel to Alice. Some, of course, called her honorable directly while smiling sweetly, and that made the sarcasm even worse. It serrated the sound of the word, giving it a stealth-like sadistic edge. It was not as if they hated her. But these people, these Nazis, were in the service of the most fanatical evil human beings on earth. The most dangerous predator. And they themselves honed their own predatory instincts on the small stuff, the less threatening. They could smell weakness, and it emboldened them.

A family of Tyrolean musicians strolled through the crowd, one with an accordion and two with fiddles.

The guests watching and applauding the music and the frivolity were the most powerful men of the Third Reich. The grotesquely fat Hermann Göring, commander of the German air force, the Luftwaffe, was clapping his hands to the music and beaming. Next to him was the minister of propaganda, Joseph Goebbels, who was as thin as Göring was fat. By Goebbels's side was his beautiful wife, Magda. Her hair was luminous in the summer sunshine, and she was the only one dressed not in a dirndl but an exquisite afternoon dress, most likely a Paris design. She would no more wear a dirndl than the Duchess of Windsor would. The only unhappy face was that of Gerda Bormann, wife of Martin Bormann, the head of the Nazi party. She was a large woman, with dark hair parted down the middle. Stuffed into a dirndl, she stood out in the festive crowd as almost defiantly unfestive. Her mouth was set in a grave line. She appeared suffused with a melancholy darkness. She was midnight in the noonday sun. The shadows of her babies and young children slid around the hem of her skirt.

Alice spied Frau Bormann's eldest daughter Irmgard, a fellow Rhine maiden.

"Hello, Irmgard. Ready for tonight? The big one, I guess?"

Irmgard looked at her blankly. "Wh-what are you talking about?"

"Act Three, 'The Ride of the Valkyries.' The Führer's favorite, I believe."

"Oh! Oh yes, of course . . . and now we are all Valkyries. I'm afraid I can't recall . . ."

"My name. Ute . . . Ute Schnaubel. The Reich Praktikum student."

"Oh yes, of course! Now I remember you."

It was close to ten o'clock in the evening before the curtain rose on the scene of "The Ride of the Valkyries." The audience gasped as the peaks of Valhalla loomed in the lavender twilight. The whirring of the fans behind the Valkyries, perched on a mountaintop, gave them the cue to spread their wings.

Was it true, Alice thought, that a half dozen swans had been slaughtered for these costumes? Why not? The Nazis were killing humans—Jews, Romá, homosexuals, and god knew who else. What was a swan or two, or a dozen for that matter? The battle cry began, and it was actually Alice who had to open her mouth first. The other Valkyries soon joined her in the battle cry. They moved the wings strapped to their arms and swooped down to retrieve a slain warrior from the battlefield. The "warriors" were in fact rag dolls with torn red scraps of material—the mortal wounds—sewn onto their bodies. The Valkyries transported them to Valhalla.

Alice glanced out from the stage. Adolf Hitler sat transfixed in the front row. His eyes were clasped on her. Was he projecting? Was he imagining himself as the slain warrior she would transport to Valhalla? Could she do what Alfred Stegall, the legendary Rasa spy, had done in the Great War? Could she stop this evil sapper from blowing up the world. The difference here was that Stegall didn't have to drive the sapper to kill himself. He merely evoked the image of the beautiful movie star and hypnotized the sapper, which allowed Stegall to defuse the explosives without ever lifting a lethal weapon with his own hand. But with the Starling it would be different. She must instill in Adolf Hitler the notion of a valiant death. She would not pull the trigger, but he must. And it was the job of a Valkyrie to ensure that this could happen.

Hitler never blinked. Not once. Eva Braun sat next to him. Her lips pressed into a plump pout of complete boredom.

The scene only lasted eight minutes. As the curtain began to slowly drop, there was a roar. The audience was in a frenzy. Hitler jumped to his feet, clapping wildly. A mad light of absolute delirium suffused his eyes. It was not human, this light. It was that of a beast, an animal gone berserk. *These are the eyeballs of hell!*

That was Alice Winfield's only thought.

Her fios, Colonel Stauffenberg, had not attended the performance this time. But she wished he could have witnessed that look in Hitler's eyes as he jumped from his seat to applaud. She had not much to compare it to, for she had not been at the Berghof that long, but just judging from those crazed luminous eyes, the Führer seemed far from stable. There had been two previous performances from Wagner's operas, but neither had received such an intense response. Was he in fact beginning to unravel with the turn in the tide of the war? It had only been ten days since the Allied invasion. But Alice imagined she saw in those mad eyes a vision of his own destruction—his own death. Or was she becoming delusional?

There was no doubt that the Allies were making advances. The tide was slowly beginning to turn. The American and British troops had launched the largest water invasion in history, and in the scant days since D-Day, they had captured Bayeux and the port of Cherbourg in France. And this came after the German rocket attack on London that they had hoped would somehow deter the onslaught of the Allies. But it had only seemed to further incite their enemy.

No one here spoke of these losses. She needed to report to her secret contact, the child named Hedwig. Tomorrow, when several of the kitchen maids were going to the lake to swim, she would go and look for her. There was a safe word that had been included in the sweet paper, so that they could identify each other. Then Alice would pass whatever information she could give to Hedwig. But certainly there had been madness in Hitler's eyes as he leaped to his feet three times in the repeat performances. Each time that light of madness grew fiercer.

She could not sleep. Suddenly hungry, she got up and made her way to the kitchen. Until she walked through the swinging door, she had completely forgotten Frau Kalhammer's words about the apple cake that the Führer often sought out in the middle of the night. And there indeed was the Führer, standing by the pastry table in a plush velvet bathrobe. How could she have forgotten?

He looked at her, somewhat confused. Was he going to ask her for apple cake? Did he call it apple cake or Führer cake? Insane questions danced a jig through Alice's mind. There was a butcher knife not eight inches from her grasp. If she grabbed it and plunged it into his belly, it might all be over. The war might end.

"Wer bist du?" he asked. Who are you? Then a merry twinkle. "Mit den Zöpfen."

Zöpfen! The braids . . . her braids. She had forgotten to unbraid her fat Valkyrie braids. "Brünnhilde!" Yes, she was, as he said, Brünnhilde! He clasped his hands now, over his heart. "You have come to save me, you dear child. Dear Brünnhilde has come to save me with some apple cake."

"Of course, mein Führer," she replied docilely.

And so she cut a slice of the cake with the dull blade of a cake knife that hung next to the butcher knife. For just a second her hand hesitated between the two knives. He asked her to stay while he ate the cake and drank the glass of apple juice she poured him. He simply stared at her the whole time. He asked her no questions. Not even her name.

She felt for some reason this was significant. It was as if he was still suspended in the fantasy of the opera. The evening was hot. A slight draft, like a sigh, blew through the open window of the kitchen. She almost felt a downy fluff of feathers stir on her arms. She must remain, in his eyes, Brünnhilde—not a Reich Praktikum student or a kitchen servant, but Brünnhilde, a Valkyrie, a chooser of the slain.

When he got up to leave, he looked at her almost pleadingly. Unspoken words hung in the still night air of the kitchen. *Auf wiedersehen bis Valhalla.* Goodbye until Valhalla.

It wasn't until Alice returned to her small room that the reality of that scene fully struck her. He had been begging her to choose him. He was, in fact, seeing her as a Valkyrie, ready to plunge down on her swan wings and lift him to

Valhalla. He was imploring to be seen in her eyes as a hero warrior.

But when she finally went to bed that night, she thought not of the Führer, or the strange fixation in his eyes as he stared at her, but of the thick slice of apple cake. How David would have loved that slice of cake! She could not wait to return and bring him cake. Not a slice, but a whole cake! Was there ever a braver child, a more heroic child, than David Bloom? Never!

NINETEEN

MORÐ, MURT, FEALLMHARÚ

In Icelandic the word is "morð." In Gaelic, "murt," and in Irish Gaelic, "feallmharú." But they all mean the same thing. For Rasas, they are all deadly. For they mean assassination.

"Ja! Ja! Christopher Columbus!" The blond little girl plunged beneath the surface of the lake and came up with the twig. From the shore of the lake they looked like two girls, one older, perhaps her sister, playing the age-old swimming game of diving after a stick. Little would anyone expect they were discussing the planned assassination attempt of Adolf Hitler.

Hedwig had melted out of the birch forest onto the path like a woodland sprite. Blond and spindly, yet a bit tall for her nine years. On the path she walked alongside Alice for perhaps ten seconds before taking her hand. "Mama said you'd watch me while I swam. I like to swim to the deep part.

I'm a very good swimmer."

"Oh, I'm sure you are," Alice replied.

"Yes, advanced level five."

That was the highest level one could attain for her age.

And so the two had met, and in that fleeting conversation had established their basic credentials.

It was not, of course, until they were several yards from shore that Hedwig uttered the word "feallmharú." Assassination.

"And when?" Alice asked casually.

"Five days after St. Morfitt's Day." The Rasa celebrated Thomas Morfitt's birthday, spymaster to King Henry VIII and the founder of the Rasas, on July 15. So July 20 was the date of the assassination.

"Here?"

"Nein, Úlfabælið," she replied in Icelandic. The language of Iceland was often used as a code language between agents.

The Wolf's Lair! Hitler's military headquarters on the Eastern Front near the town of Rastenburg.

They swam back to shore together. On the beach, Hedwig's mother was waiting. She waved to the girls as they came ashore.

"Good swim?" she asked her daughter, and wrapped her in a towel. Then she turned to Alice and smiled broadly. "You are a good girl to look out for Hedwig. She is an excellent swimmer, but she likes to swim far, and I don't want her to go out to the middle of the lake by herself. Thank you."

She paused a moment. "Thank you for everything."

"Ah, think nothing of it."

Alice took the towel, dried off, and began to walk back.

"Good luck!" the woman said softly.

"Bye-bye," Hedwig called.

Alice had only been back ten minutes when there was a knock on her door.

"Yes?"

"Fräulein, may I come in? I have an urgent message." It was Frau Kalhammer, the head housekeeper.

"Yes, of course." Alice opened the door. She had a towel wrapped around her wet hair. "Just back from the lake, swimming."

"Oh, that's nice, but I'm afraid it's your last one for a while. You are to head back to Berlin within the hour. You will have a few days there." She made a slight grimace. "No opera there, just serving the officers and perhaps working to assist Frau Traudl Junge."

"Who?"

"The Führer's private secretary. Oh! You haven't met her yet?"

"No, ma'am."

"Traudl is the Führer's principal secretary. Very nice woman. But now, of course, Fräulein Braun is in a twit, as she is not going to Rastenburg, but Traudl is and so are you!"

"Me?" Alice asked innocently.

"Yes, he asked for the girl who played Brünnhilde. He couldn't quite remember your name or, for that matter, that you are a Reich Praktikum scholar. But then again, he has a lot on his mind."

"First I have to go in advance and make sure all is ready." She sighed.

Good! thought Alice. She would have time to see her parents, and David and perhaps see the girl who she had mistaken for her sister. She remembered the exact corner. It was a popular stretch with cafés and shops. But of course, since the Allied bombings, who knew if the cafés were still there? There were always throngs of troops striding about in their tan uniforms and red swastika armbands. Not a pleasant thought. But if she could get a glimpse of that girl, it would be worth threading her way through those thugs.

Alice was assigned to ride in car number eleven of the motorcade that would convey the Führer, his closest officers, and perhaps a dozen others from the Berghof household to the special train that would take them to Berlin.

Flanking the motorcade on either side were BMW R75 motorcycles.

She sat between other girls, who were chatting amiably about how cute the motorcycle soldiers were. One leaned across Alice to look out the window.

"Try to see their badges?" She began to lower her window.

"Nein! Nein!" shrieked Hans. "That is not permitted!"

"But we're sweltering back here," Hannah said.

"Sorry, young ladies. I'll turn on the air fans. Wouldn't want your pretty faces to get sweaty."

"Aaach!" The two girls made disgusted sounds.

"Keep your thoughts to yourself, old man," Hannah said.

"Farty head," muttered Ulla. "Oh, I can see this fellow's sleeve." The car had slowed as they wound through a village. "My, my, what a strange symbol on the badge."

"What does it look like?"

"Sort of like an anchor," Ulla replied. "Maybe the navy?"

Hannah now leaned across Alice for a better look. "Pardon me, but what's your name again? I feel I should know you."

Of course she should. They had stood side by side as Rhine maidens onstage.

Alice smiled slightly. "I was Flosshilde in the first act we did."

"Oh yes, of course." Both girls giggled.

"How stupid of us," Ulla said. "I think you just have one of those faces."

"Oooh, look, we're stopping! I can get a really good look now." Ulla emitted a small gasp. "Not an anchor. It looks like an animal trap. My father hunts. He has traps like those."

"A Wolfsanker." Hans, the driver, chimed in. "A meat hook."

"Oh ja . . . ja," the two girls muttered. They had all seen parts of that symbol incorporated into many badges. Often it had been like a crescent moon shape or sometimes wings. But now it just looked like a cruel trap.

Three or four minutes had passed without the motorcade moving.

"Why have we stopped?" Ulla asked.

Then they heard a bark. Ahead, a door slammed and a dog on a leash jumped out with an officer following.

"Uh-oh!" Hans said as Eva Braun followed. She was screaming at the top of her lungs while a small woman with her hair skinned back in a bun began to mop her skirt with a towel.

"Jesus Christus," Ulla moaned. "Blondi threw up again."

A minute later Liesl Ostertag stuck her head in the open door.

"Hello, ladies. I'm afraid the honorable Fräulein Braun and I shall be riding with you the rest of the way to the train station."

"Oh noooo!" they all three moaned.

"Don't worry, she doesn't stink. I poured lavender water on her skirt." She then turned to Alice. "And who is this lovely young lady?"

"Ute Schnaubel. I brought Fräulein Braun the magazines."

"Oh yes, of course, Now I remember. You are the RP scholar. I haven't seen you around lately."

"She was Brünnhilde in the performance the other night," Hannah offered.

"Yes, of course. But you're not wearing your braids now."

Eva Braun climbed into the car. Her face was tearstained. "He makes my little darlings, Stasi and Negus, ride in crates, and yet it's Blondi who vomits all over everything. It's not fair."

"There, there," Frau Ostertag soothed her. "Here, take a drop of this." She pulled out a small vial from a satchel. "This will help."

Eva Braun's anger seemed to melt away. She looked lovingly at her maid. "You, dear Liesl, are the only one who truly understands me." Eva put her head on Liesl's shoulder.

Alice studied Eva's face. Her mouth seemed to be in a permanent pout. Alice would not call her dumb, but simply devoid of any real thoughts. Thoughtless as a dim little minor planet circling a sun.

Alice leaned back in her seat. The lavender water did little to relieve the smell of dog vomit. Ulla cracked her window a bit. Hans did not seem to mind. Alice put her head back against the seat. She remembered once when she and Louise were driving back from Rasa camp after their parents had picked them up. She had become carsick and thrown up all over Louise. They pulled off the road at a spot that was close to a babbling creek. The day was beastly hot.

"I know what to do," Louise cried out. "Let's go swimming in our clothes and wash out all the throw-up." And so they did. To dry off, they rolled themselves in the clover of a nearby meadow.

It all came back to Alice now, the delicious feeling of

swimming in the creek. Her sister's face . . . the one she knew so well. And then that face in the crowd. That scent in the bakery. Was this some terrible joke? She felt as if she was being cruelly teased with these memories. She must look for her sister. But which sister? Which face? Her head drooped. She was on the brink of sleep but woke as the car stopped once again, this time at the station where the special Führer train awaited them.

All fifty people boarded the train quickly and found their assigned compartments.

"Thank god!" Hannah sighed as they all sank into the upholstered seats of the compartment they would share for the rest of the trip to Berlin. "Are you going on to the Wolf's Lair?

"I believe that is the plan."

"Not me! I get to see my boyfriend, Frank!"

"You get a break?" Ulla asked.

"I do indeed." A blush crept across Hannah's face.

"No!" Ulla cried out. "You're not!"

"I believe I am."

"Am what?" Alice asked. The girls burst into a gale of giggles.

"Pregnant, silly." For a moment Alice was confused. Silly for what—not knowing or not being delighted at this announcement?

But of course—the Fount of Life, she knew of this. It was the program that rewarded young German women for giving birth.

"Yes, Frank and I both passed the purity tests and shall soon be married. He has to go to the front, but I'm to go to the Lebensborn home, where the crème de la crème of expectant mothers go. We're treated like princesses during our confinement." She now turned to Alice. "Isn't it fantastic?"

It was unthinkable for Alice at this moment. "I . . . I . . . ," she began hesitantly. "I think you must have a very strong stomach not to have thrown up with the smell of the dog vomit."

Ulla and Hannah burst into peals of laughter.

Everything, Alice thought, *everything is turned upside down and backward in this country. It's all so wrong.*

And then they were back in Berlin. When they drove out of the train station, the city appeared ghostly and shrouded in a strange gray mist. The latest bombing raids had left their mark. There were the skeletal remains of several buildings. Those left standing had been cordoned off with signs that announced that the sidewalks were closed: Warning: These Buildings Are Unsafe to Walk Near. Darkened and charred, the ruined buildings loomed threateningly behind a scrim of ashes. To Alice they seemed like an invasion of zombies.

At last, Alice stepped out of the car.

"And who are you?" The plump apple-cheeked woman peered at Alice.

"Ute. Remember me?"

"Oh . . . oh yes . . . the RP girl. Must be all that time in the healthy air of the mountains." She was chattering nonstop. "But now I remember that a message came in about you. You can have a break until the Führer goes to the Wolf's Lair."

"She gets to go, and I don't!" Eva Braun's piercing voice split the air as she stomped off.

TWENTY

IN SO MANY WORDS

"Downstairs, Fräulein. Downstairs!" Walter, the top mechanic under her father, pointed at the floor. "With the recent bombings, the apartment was no longer safe." He pointed to a heavy metal door. "And be careful on the steps."

It was a long spiraling staircase. At the bottom was another door. She could see a seam of light beneath it, and she heard some music. She knocked on the door.

"Ja ja . . . ich komme." It was her mother. There was almost a chime-like quality to her voice when she spoke German. The door opened.

"My goodness . . . my goodness," Posie Winfield kept exclaiming. "She's back, Gunther. Our Ute is back." Her mother embraced her fiercely. She wished just once she could be called Alice again. It was as if she felt herself an imposter

184

in her mother's arms. Then her father came. His long arms encircled them both.

"We know! We know." Her mother pressed her mouth to her ear as they embraced.

"Not too long, maybe it will all be over." Her father was muttering close to her other ear. "All together again!"

Louise's face flashed in her mind. And her mum was cautioning her father not to count one's chickens before they hatched.

The apartment in the basement was smaller and dimmer and had a slightly damp smell mixed with that of oil. Her father told them that this was where he had lived during the worst of the bombing of Berlin, right before Alice and Posie had arrived. Moving down again was no problem, as the apartment had already been set up. This most recent bombing was nothing apparently compared to the autumn of the year before in 1943, when more than two thousand people had been killed in Berlin.

When they settled down around the small kitchen table for some tea, her father took out a money clip with some reichsmarks. "You'll need some warm clothes, as it can get cold there even in July, and rainy." She didn't reject the money, although she knew she could buy all these items without cash at the department store where the Führer's household had an account. What she planned to do was to buy clothes for David. She was as determined to see David Bloom on this trip and to bring him a whole cake, an apple cake, as she was to search for her sister.

In the conversation it became clear her parents already knew about their daughter's impending trip to the Wolf's Lair and also what was to transpire. Rasa agents were keenly intuitive. In just a few words they could communicate with a degree of fluency that others could never aspire to. They asked about her time away, and she told them of her performances.

"The Führer was quite charmed with me in the role of Brünnhilde, I believe." Then she added, "Of course he could not remember my name or who I was a bit later." Both her parents nodded knowingly, with pride.

"Perfect," her mother whispered. In short, she was "on mission." Posie sensed that what her daughter had just said was a key element to her mission.

In so many words—words that were not quite in normal context—much information was exchanged. But Alice did have one question that she wanted answered—those motor-cycle riders with the badges of the wolf trap.

"Oh, those," her mother replied. "Just a moment, dear." Posie went over to the gramophone and put on a record. The music was earthshaking.

Posie Winfield began to speak in a low voice. "So the wolf trap badge is the insignia of a new German resistance force, part of a new plan. The new force is to carry out guerrilla attacks against occupying forces."

"Occupying?" Alice opened her eyes wide.

"The Russians aren't falling back. They're closer every day. Not only that, but new units are being formed. A militia, the Volkssturm. Old men and even children are being armed. Can you believe it? Children! They are sending children out there with guns and grenades. They hardly have any guns left since the Russians blew up those factories to the south."

"But what does that symbol of the wolf trap mean?"

"It's one of these new units, a force known as the Werewolf . . . real brutes. They make the SS look like puppy dogs."

"But why the uniform if they're guerrilla fighters? Guerrilla fighters, resistance fighters, don't normally wear uniforms, right?"

"Psychological, my dear. Most likely the P of D."

Alice instantly knew who they were referring to. The P of D, the Prince of Darkness. It was code for Joseph Goebbels, the master of propaganda. He was brilliant at the game of intimidation, through which he could manipulate a single person's mind or that of an entire population.

So, pocketing the Reichsmarks her father gave her, an hour later Alice left the garage. She didn't go immediately to the department store, but stopped first at Kaiser Wilhelm Memorial Church and the mailbox on the southeast corner of the Breitscheidplatz. There she left a chalk mark, to signal to the operative that she would be leaving a coded message at the dead drop location in the hedge of the church's cemetery.

The message was an assessment of the Führer's mental condition. Her report was brief. The code was a triplex—Icelandic with inverted vowels and mathematical symbols.

Physical and mental condition appear to have deteriorated noticeably in last ten days. Tremor in arm markedly worse. Sleeping only one to two hours at night, according to people close to him. Mumbles incessantly to himself. Easily distracted, except when watching scenes from his favorite operas. Irritability increased. I suggest that Starling is increasingly susceptible to reverse projection phenomena.

She had written on an old newspaper in a code where she had circled certain words. It was Rasa code four six five that she had used to encode. She dropped the message, and her contact—whoever that was—would use Rasa code five six four to decode it.

She then headed toward the department store Hermankrantz. It was the only department store, now that the Jewish one, Wertheim, had been taken over by the Reich.

But before she went to the store, she walked to the block where she first had glimpsed Louise, or the girl who she thought was Louise. She stood on the corner and scanned the throngs of people. There were several young men with the badges of the wolf trap that those motorcycle troopers had worn. But there was no sign of Louise. Alice realized that this could be a fruitless effort. There were more than three million people in Berlin. The chances of her sister's new or old face showing up were ridiculously slim. Perhaps on some level she had subconsciously been wishing to see her sister and had willed her face to appear.

Her thoughts went back to her mission. She knew that she would not be the actual agent to pull the trigger. Or would it be poison? Or a bomb? She would be an inoperative accessory at best, as opposed to a special op. Her job was to stay alert and serve as a passive conduit. She must be able to maintain the highest level of vigilance and also absolute deniability of any knowledge.

Apparently the Allied air forces had been boosted by the invasion in Normandy that had happened only three weeks before. Their strategic bombing on Berlin had wreaked more destruction than she had thought. The central part of the city, the Mitte, was severely damaged, along with a train station, from strategic bombing on factories and supply depots. There were gouges in the street, exposing the innards of the city. Along with tangles of electrical wires, there was the stench of ruptured sewer lines. It was as if some surgeon from the sky had decided to operate and rip out a devouring cancer. But the cancer was only spreading. The air was so thick with dust that Alice had to wrap her scarf around her mouth so she would not inhale the soot and grime of war.

* * *

The department store where she had planned to buy warm clothes was almost completely demolished. A woman ran from the ruins clutching a bundle of some sort.

"Help yourself, darling! It's drenched with water, but it will dry out." It looked as if she was carrying blankets and possibly jackets. Was it considered looting if the goods were damaged? Alice thought she might as well try. She found no clothing, damaged or otherwise, but she did find several cans of tinned goods in the food section, similar to Harrod's department store in London. Food would be better than blankets, at least for now. She stuffed her shopping satchel with half a dozen tins of sardines and three smaller ones of liver pate. *Where'd the liver come from?* she wondered. She hoped not a pig. But then again, David himself had bought the pork sausage when his father had ordered him to leave train station.

This part of the city smelled like wet ashes, but the odor diminished as she headed north and east toward the alley of the whipped-cream house. She passed Zeiberg's Bakery, where she and her mother had first bought the bee sting cake and the baker had given her some cookies as a welcome gift to the neighborhood. Now there were no elaborate goodies in the window—just bread. Nevertheless, she went through the door. The bell tinkled. The proprietor looked up.

"Welcome. I wish I had more to offer. But just bread, child."

"Bread will be fine."

"You must be new to the neighborhood. Haven't seen you around before."

"Yes, um . . . I was evacuated during the bombings in autumn. . . ."

"Came back just in time for a second round for summer, eh?"

"Guess so."

"Great timing." He gave a gruff laugh. "Normally I offer a gift of our special anise cookies. But you tell me where I can find anise these days?"

"It's okay, I'll just take that." She pointed at a seeded loaf of bread.

"Good choice. The healthiest bread that I make."

"Oh, good, very good." Alice took the reichsmarks from her pocket and paid for the bread.

TWENTY-ONE

THE SECRET GARDEN

The whipped-cream house still stood, as elegant as ever. Alice leaned against a lamppost watching it. There was no sign of life, however. No official cars pulled up in front. The housemaids were probably inside dusting, waxing floors, and polishing silver. It seemed so odd. How could the world go on like this, with the war raging outside its walls? The house was within three quarters of a mile from the bombed-out blocks she had just left. Perhaps it was like during the German bombing campaign of London—the Blitz, it was called. There were massive air raids against the city. Many died. Buildings and homes were left in smithereens. For fifty-seven days and nights, London was pounded. But despite all, London managed to carry on.

She remembered three years before, at the beginning of the

Blitz, when they were living in Eaton Square. The maids had came and dusted and polished. In this instance, her mother had posed as a war widow with distinguished ancestry. Of course, it was all set up by the Company and MI6. The cover story was their family's aristocratic history—complete with fabricated documentation, as well as the house bought and furnished by MI6.

Posie Winfield carried this off so well that some people had thought she should, perhaps postwar, become a lady-in-waiting for King George VI's wife, the queen. In her role Posie had performed beautifully and uncovered a double agent— the Duchess of Chatsworth, a close friend of the despicable Duke and Duchess of Windsor, who had been great admirers of Hitler. The Duchess of Chatsworth had been sent to the London Cage in Kensington, a prison and facility for interrogating spies during the war.

And life went on for Posie, Alice, and Louise in their elegant Eaton Square home until they moved to the country. Although the girls' father, Alan Winfield, was far away, and even though bombs were dropping, they were cozy, the three of them. Until Louise had to go to Norway to map the heavy water plant—the nuclear reactors that the Nazis were developing. Heavy water was anything but just plain water. It had been treated so that it would become a key ingredient for atomic weapons. They called it heavy because it contained a larger amount of hydrogen. A special kind of hydrogen.

If Alice ever got back to Rasa camp and had the advanced physics course, she would learn more about it. And then she too might be called upon to map a secret nuclear facility. When she tried to compare what she had learned in Rasa camp with what she had learned at the stupid Hermann von Haupt Gymnasium, it was simply ridiculous.

What a celebration the three Winfields had in 1943 when British troops and Norwegian guerrillas crossed the mountain plateaus and finally succeeded in blowing up the plant that Louise had so carefully mapped. What Louise had done was heroic. Of course the Company could never celebrate such heroes publicly. And now Louise was out of the Company.

It had been a quiet celebration—for that was how spies must celebrate. Nevertheless, the director of the Company did come to see them and brought heartiest congratulations from Maxwell Knight, head of MI6. And now Louise was out of the game. Or was she? What kind of game might she be playing, if indeed the girl Alice had spied was her sister?

She heard a door slam, the front door of the house. It was the maid who Alice had seen before, the one who had served the officers in the garden. She watched her turn the corner and head in the opposite direction, away from the alley. As soon as she was out of sight, Alice walked calmly, nonchalantly, to the alley. Her heart was beating hard. Would David still be there? She had been gone a number of weeks. Not much could have happened to him since then—or could it? Could he have been discovered in his indoor hiding place, the secret space in the cellar? The weather had been warm. Perhaps he didn't always have to be there all night long. And would he recognize her? He always had, for some reason that she could not fathom. But now it had been so long.

The fully leafed branches of the trees that bordered the alley formed a green canopy. Dappled sunlight trickled through the leafy embroidery. It was a green veil, so unlike the scrim of ashes in the other parts of Berlin. Slinging her satchel over her shoulder, she reached for the low branch of the tree neighboring the one where David usually perched. She heard a soft trill. She paused to listen. It came again. Some sort of bird. Then nothing. She waited. There was a stream of soft giggles, very human giggles, falling through the leaves. She looked up.

"David!" His dark luminous eyes seemed almost too big for his face, which was paler and thinner than when she had last seen him. He swung down to the branch where she was perched.

"You heard the bird?"

"I thought it was a bird."

"You thought wrong. It was me." He smiled and made the sound again. "You know which bird?"

"No idea."

"A barred owl."

"But it's not a hoot. Owls hoot."

David sighed and rolled his eyes. "Common misconception. It's as silly as saying all humans speak German. No, they do not all hoot. There are as many different owl sounds as there are species of owl—of which there are hundreds." He pursed his lips, and a staccato of peeping noises issued forth. "A pygmy owl." He launched into a demonstration for the next few minutes, until Alice held up her hand.

"Are you hungry?"

"Not really."

This was a bad sign, Alice knew. People who were starving often became inured, desensitized to their own hunger.

"But you must be. You're . . . you're too thin."

"A lot of people have left. Not much garbage. One grows used to it."

"You shouldn't grow used to it."

David looked her with the strangest expression. As if to say, "You poor thing. You know so little."

"Here, I've brought some food for you." She took out the bread and handed it to him. He began to tear off a piece. "You like sardines?"

"Sure," he replied.

She lifted the tiny metal key that was soldered to the lid and began to peel back the top. The tiny sardines were neatly lined up. He picked one and put it on top of the bread and was about to pop it into his mouth, then began to mutter words under his breath.

"Baruch atah Adonai, Eloheinu Melech ha-olam, asher

196

kid'shanu b'mitzvotav v'tzivanu l'hadlik ner shel Shabbat."
He stopped suddenly and looked at her. "Is it Friday? Shabbat?"

"Uh . . . no. It's Tuesday."

"No matter," he continued. Then he smiled. "Baruch
atah, Ute." He looked up at Alice. "Bless you, Ute."

He began eating the bread with the sardines.

"I brought some more stuff. Here in the satchel. I wanted
to bring an apple cake, but they didn't have one."

"It's okay. This is good." He swallowed. "I didn't realize how hungry I was." He tipped his head toward the trash
bins. "They used to throw out more, but now not much. No
waste." He continued eating. "You said it's Tuesday?"

"Yes."

"That's good. It means the maid might be away."

"I saw the maid leave by the front door."

"Great!"

"Why? What do you want to show me? Something in the
house?"

"Oh no. The garden."

"We can go down there? No one will see us."

She glanced toward the terrace where the officers had
been drinking champagne.

"Not there. Tuesday afternoon is the servants' day off.
I can show you something." He paused. "The secret part."
Alice's eyes opened wide.

* * *

They had moved to another tree nearby. Perched over a separate part of the garden, Alice looked down. Beneath her was a flotilla of lilies of the valley, their tiny bell-like heads nodding, their chimes perhaps heard only by two butterflies that swooped past on their way to a stand of foxgloves. Violets crept along a narrow path, occasionally interrupted by the bright yellow of a lady's slipper—the most elusive of woodland plants, only rarely found in cultivated gardens. There were also trembling toad lilies, shyly tipping their blue and pink faces toward a narrow slant of sunshine.

What was not in the garden was as important as what *was* there in the other part of the garden, the nonsecret part. There were no roses that announced themselves in bright scrambles on trellises. No bursts of immense lilies, statuesque and brilliant, with their movie-star blossoms of arresting beauty. No irises, dignified and proud, in hues of royal purples and commanding scarlets. Nor were there clusters of pansies or squabbling petunias. This garden was wild and wandering, ambling quietly through the shadows and only seeking the occasional beam of sunlight that dropped through the green veil.

"What are those evergreen trees over there with the droopy branches? They look like they're crying."

David laughed. "Well, actually they are called weeping pines. But they kind of remind me of old rabbis. Some had long beards that swayed while praying, like the one I was learning Torah from for my bar mitzvah. We all began our bar mitzvah studies early because all Jewish children were expelled from public schools. Before my studies were completely interrupted by the Nazis." He paused. "You know about bar mitzvahs, don't you?"

"Of course." Alice laughed.

"But here's something I bet you don't know."

"What's that?"

"Even in winter, certain things bloom in this garden. Winter bloom, my mother called it."

"What kinds of flowers bloom in winter?"

"More than you might suspect. Hellebores, quince, heather—all kinds of flowers. So you like this secret garden?" David whispered.

"I love it. It's . . . it's so wild. It just rambles." She was searching for other words. "It's not . . ."

"Not what?"

"Spick-and-span." The words were from her favorite book, *The Secret Garden*.

"Spick-and-span?" David asked.

Alice turned to him. His face had changed. There was a new brightness in his eyes.

"It's from a book that I read a long time ago. There was a boy and a girl who helped bring a garden back to life. And the boy, named Dickon, said he wouldn't want a gardener's garden. All clipped and spick-and-span. That gardens are nice when things were running wild."

There was a sudden gust of wind. A smile broke across

199

David's face. "Look at that!" He pointed at a tree where a stand of ferns at its base suddenly snagged and the vines of white flowers clambered up a tree. "Those vines caught hold just like my mother said they would."

"Oh, those are lovely. What kind of flower?"

"A star clematis. Very rare. She found it in the woods near our summer home. My mum wasn't sure it would grow here."

"But it did!" Alice exclaimed.

"And she never saw it," he said softly. Alice turned her head. She couldn't look at him. There was a silence—the silence of profound grief.

TWENTY-TWO

THE SWEET TASTE OF DEATH

The night before she was to leave for the Wolf's Lair, Alice leaned against the open garage door and watched as lightning flashed in the sky. "Sounds like the 'Anvil Chorus' up there!" her father said, putting a hand on her shoulder. "Better come in. It's going to be torrential."

Wind tore through the city, and just across the way, two shutters ripped from a building and clattered to the street. But Alice was still engulfed in that silence of David's grief. She thought of that pale yet somehow luminous face. She remembered the first time she had seen him. She had thought he resembled a changeling from one of her fairy-tale books. What would happen to him tonight? She hoped he was inside. The air had turned chilly. Then a downpour began. *He'll be cold.*

"Who will be cold?" her father asked. She was sure that she hadn't spoken out loud. "Oh . . . oh . . . nothing . . . just a cat I saw this afternoon. That's all."

"Believe me, cats are going to survive this world more than humans. The Russians have just destroyed the German Fourth Army, along with the Panzer units. I think they'll be here by March."

"Really, Papa? But what about us?"

"I'm thinking, dear. I'm thinking." Was he thinking about Louise? How often Alice had been tempted to tell her parents of that sighting near the newsstand. That girl whose face floated out of the crowd. She could almost see it now, like an image in a disturbing dream. A dream that was not really a nightmare, but so disturbing still. As if her mind was being torn apart.

Thinking meant he was planning. A strategy of some sort was most likely in the works. Timing would be everything. And it would depend on a lot of spy work and high-quality intel. And that was exactly why she had to do her job. She had already received a sweet paper concerning the planned assassination, the Feallmharù, as they were calling it. The last bits of the paper had dissolved in her mouth hours ago.

The trip to the headquarters on the Eastern Front would be a long one. She would use the time to review every bit of information that she had read and then eaten.

She could not help but think of Mr. Churchill. She recalled so vividly how she and her mum and her father had gathered

202

around the wireless for Mr. Churchill's first address as Prime Minister. Britain had declared war on Germany just eight months before, two days after the Germans' invasion of Poland. And things were not going well. The Nazis march to the west seemed inevitable. On the evening of May 19, 1940, the radio crackled and then the BBC News reader's voice came on. "Ladies and gentlemen, the next voice you shall hear will be our prime minister, Winston Churchill." The slightly nasal voice of the prime minister issued forth.

"I speak to you for the first time as Prime Minister in a solemn hour for the life of our country, of our empire, of our Allies, and above all, of the cause of freedom. A tremendous battle is raging in France and Flanders. The Germans, by a remarkable combination of air bombing and heavily armored tanks, have broken through the French defenses . . ."

His speech built to a crescendo as he called upon countries to rescue "not only Europe but mankind from the foulest and most soul-destroying tyranny which has ever darkened and stained the pages of history."

For eight minutes he spoke. Her father had embraced them. It was as if Alice could still feel his fingers gripping her shoulder. She was only ten years old then. Barely up to her father's shoulder. Then the prime minister finally came to those fierce, final words, the clarion call to honor, to courage—to valor.

"Arm yourselves, and be ye men of valour, and be in readiness for the conflict; for it is better for us to perish in battle than to look upon the outrage of our nation and our altar. As the will of God is in heaven, even so let it be."

Now, four years later, less than half a mile from the very center of that foul and soul-destroying tyranny of Adolf Hitler, Alice Winfield stood tall beside her father and thought, *I am a girl of valor and almost a woman. I shall do all I can do to help that man of valor, my fios, Claus von Stauffenberg, code name Wotan, fulfill his mission. So help me God.*

TWENTY-THREE
THE WOLF'S JAWS

Alice had boarded the train at midnight, along with perhaps seventy-five others of the Hitler's entourage. For close to ten hours, the Führer's train snaked through the gloomy forests of East Germany. It was a moonless night in mid-July, and their departure time was critical. It must be dark with no moon. The inky night was still scattered with pinpricks of light. But they were prepared in case of a devastating attack by the British aircraft. Mounted on each end of the train were four-barrel guns that could fire twenty-millimeter shells if attacked.

The train was in fact a perfect target for an assassination attempt, according to her father. Thus far there had been more than twenty attempts to assassinate Hitler since 1937. But this one planned for the Wolf's Lair had to work. *Tap wood,* Alice thought, and lightly touched her fingers to the armrest of her seat in the train. *Stupid! Magical thinking!* She remembered her mum's reprimand once to Louise about such nonsense, when her sister had showed her a rabbit foot someone had given her for good luck.

"Ridiculous!" their mother had hooted. Then her voice had dropped to a throaty whisper. "Listen to me, daughters. Rasas have no time for such nonsense. Sharp thinking, logic, stealth, and planning—that is what we do. And that is why we're the best spies in the world."

So now Alice reviewed the plan and the further information that she had learned about the layout of the Wolf's Lair. Her fios, Stauffenberg, would arrive on July 19. That was almost three days away. During that time, she must learn the lay of the land. She focused on the crude map that had been sketched for her on the sweet paper. Other sweet papers had followed, laying out additional details of the headquarters.

The Wolf's Lair was the least accessible of all the Führer's headquarters. It was deep within a forest. It had been laid out in three concentric circles. Each of these circles constituted a security zone. The innermost circle was zone one. This was where Hitler's bunker and his highest-ranking ministers stayed. Zone two surrounded the inner zone and housed several of the Reich ministers and military personnel. Zone three, the outermost zone, was the most heavily fortified, with dozens of land mines. This was the realm of the Führer Brigade, a special armored security unit.

In all, there were thirty-two different buildings and sites. Alice had memorized them and knew each one's function, from Hitler's sleeping bunker to the barracks of the press secretary to radio and telex buildings, in addition to a tearoom and movie theater. *After all, it was necessary to be entertained while destroying the world,* Alice thought.

Alice herself was to be housed in a building called the Cottage, with others of the domestic staff.

She felt confident that she could find her way through the Wolf's Lair at any time, even in the dead of night. That was not to say that if there were a crisis and she needed to leave quickly she could do so without being blown up. The intelligence she got was not "super granular," a term used by Rasas for the highest and most complete level of information. So she still did not know the specific locations of the fifty land mines buried just outside the security zone.

Stauffenberg, or Wotan, would be arriving in a few days close to noon. He would almost immediately join Hitler in the presentation room for a conference. Beneath the shirt of his uniform, Wotan would have explosives taped to his chest. But it was not a suicide mission. In order for the bomb to be activated, he had to execute several small steps.

The first thing he had to do was remove himself from the X-Zone, in Rasa language—the place of the intended explosion. He would ask if he might freshen up. He would then excuse himself with his briefcase. In the restroom he would go into a stall, untape the explosives and insert the time pencil that would trigger the bomb, and then put the bomb in his briefcase. He would then return to the conference room and set the briefcase with the bomb under the conference table.

Someone would then enter the conference room and say an urgent call had just come in for Colonel Stauffenberg. It would not be Alice who delivered this message. There needed to be as much distance as possible between her and her fios, Wotan. There was obviously another operative inside who would do this final piece of work.

As dawn neared, the train began to slow. And it was perhaps when she caught that first glimmer of light that she remembered that, in fact, this day was her birthday! She had turned fourteen! Silently in her head she began to sing. . . . *Happy birthday to me . . . happy birthday to me!*

She spied the station platform ahead, and five minutes later, with the birthday song still scurrying through her mind, she disembarked.

A motorcade of cars met them. This time there were several men on motorcycles, all bearing the symbol of the wolf traps. Werewolf seemed appropriate for the Wolf's Lair, Alice thought. One of the men on a motorcycle dismounted and walked ahead several yards, then returned. He tapped on the glass of the window. The young woman sitting beside Alice rolled the window down. He stuck his head in.

"Hello, lovely ladies." He was extremely handsome and had deep blue eyes and nearly white-blond hair. She had never seen hair so blond. It was almost silver. "It appears that a herd of cows is crossing the road ahead, and we shall be detained a bit. Not long." He sighed. "But as long as we're here, we might introduce ourselves and get to know each other better. I'm Fritz, and who are you?"

"I'm Gerda."

"I'm Margot."

"Ute."

"And what may I ask brings you to the Wolf's Lair?"

There was an awkward pause. Gerda and Margot were tasters. It seemed that the Führer had an obsession with being poisoned, and ten young women had been employed by the Reich to taste all the food served to the Führer. They would eat; then, if twenty minutes had passed and they had not become ill or dropped dead, the food would be served. Alice couldn't help but wonder, how would they answer the Werewolf's question? How would they explain their tasks as tasters, ready to die for the Führer? Margot, a lovely looking young woman in her early twenties, said simply, "We're part of the kitchen staff."

Of course, Alice thought. *Perfect answer.* Sometimes she really overthought things.

Fritz's eyes sparkled. "Well, my compliments to you. I hear the food served at the Führer's table is the best. So I imagine you get some of the leftovers. *Leftovers! Hah!* thought Alice. He then tipped his helmet as rakishly as one could tip a helmet and smiled broadly. "Bon appétit!" he exclaimed, and

209

roared off on his motorcycle. It would be another forty-five minutes before they passed through the gates of the Wolf's Lair.

Against a pinkening sky the watchtower of the compound rose. They came to the first checkpoint and were waved through unceremoniously. No stopping. It seemed casual, yet here they were among Hitler's household staff. His private secretary, one of his many doctors, two new chefs, and oddly enough, Winifred Wagner! The show must go on!

And the show did go on. On Alice's first morning at the Wolf's Lair, Winifred Wagner, the opera director who had directed the performances at the Berghof, was now bustling into the kitchen. So even here the Führer needed his music.

"Actung!" she announced in a bellowing voice. "As you know, Il Duce, our dear compatriot in this war, Benito Mussolini, is a guest this evening, and the Führer wishes to have some entertainment. I'm here to recruit some actresses and actors for tonight's performance. We shall be doing excerpts from the Ring cycle. Don't worry, you do not have to do much—not sing, not dance. We have all the records. You just need to follow instructions. We did several performances a few weeks ago. But many of those people are not here now. The Görings' daughter was in several, as were Herr Bormann's many children. However, they are not available now, and there was one girl in particular who pleased the Führer very much, who was part of the staff. So I came to see if she might be here." Her eyes cast over the ten or so girls, including some of the tasters in the kitchen. They slid right over Alice's face, even though she was standing right in front of her. "Some thought she might have been an RP girl. Is that possible?"

"Yes, Frau Wagner." Alice raised her hand slightly. "I am a Reich Praktikum student."

"Ach! Right in front of me! However did I miss you?" She drew closer, until their noses were almost touching. Alice observed that one nostril had a slight scar. Childhood accident. She also had an unbecoming hair growing out of the corner of her mouth. Frau Wagner should pluck it. Maybe she couldn't see it. She was now squinting quite hard at Alice, as if to take in every detail of her face. Then slowly she said, "It's so odd. I can't remember your face at all. You might be the girl."

"Oh, I think I was that girl," Alice reassured her.

Now Frau Wagner grasped her hand. "Yes, you must have been." She gave a tight little smile. "My memory is not what it used to be. But I know that when you put on the horned helmet and wings, I'll say, 'That is Brünnhilde, chooser of the slain.' The most important of the Valkyries. Ready to wear your wings, dearie?" Alice nodded and smiled. "Then it's off to Valhalla!" She giggled. Then her face went blank again as she turned to Alice. "But now what is your name again?"

"Ute Schnaubel." Alice thought, *Ute Schnaubel, Rasa*

spy, defender of the British Empire. Ready to perish in battle rather than look upon the outrage of our nation by the likes of you and your Führer. And for that I shall fight with blood, toil, sweat, and tears against this monstrous tyranny. Mr. Churchill's words flowed through Alice and heated her blood. But no one would ever know what was surging through Alice's mind, for she had the calmest, sweetest expression on her face—one of complete innocence and submission. Yet at this moment Alice Winfield was potentially deadlier than any poisons the tasters might detect.

TWENTY-FOUR

TO TRAP A WOLF

"May I help, Frau Bender?" Alice asked as she entered the kitchen. She had been in the Wolf's Lair three days now. She was intent on making herself useful, so she often volunteered for small tasks in the kitchen beyond her regular jobs of serving tea, participating in the evening entertainments from the Ring cycle, and gathering flowers from the few beds planted between zones one and two. It turned out that Alice had a knack for flower arrangements.

"Oh yes, be a dear," said the cook. "I'm a bit late with this second sandwich platter. More in attendance than we expected. Can you take it across to the conference room?"

"Certainly," Alice replied.

"Such a dear you are. What's your name again?"

"Ute."

"Yes, Ute, take that platter over there."

A high voice piped up. "The ones with the toothpicks are for the Führer."

"I already sent those over, Fräulein Wolk."

Fräulein Wolk was a young, pretty woman who was one of perhaps a dozen of Hitler's tasters.

"Here's the platter, dear," Frau Bender said as she placed a sprig of parsley for decoration. Alice took it and walked across the courtyard to the conference room.

No one acknowledged her as she entered. Hitler was at the head of the table and seemed to stare right through her as she set the platter down on the heavy oak table. But the Führer was there. That was important. The previous attempts had been aborted because he had not been in attendance as the conspirators thought he would be.

Now Alice's only task was to confirm his presence. As she walked across the courtyard with the platter, she knew she was being watched. She had not seen him yet. But now as she exited the conference room, she saw the figure she had hoped to see crossing the courtyard. It was 12:05, and the countdown now began. Wotan was here!

He was carrying the briefcase in the only hand he had. The empty sleeve of the missing arm blew in the wind. Erect, proud, and determined, he was the very image of a high-ranking, celebrated officer of the German army. He was accompanied by his own personal assistant, Lieutenant

Werner von Haeften. Alice and the colonel passed within five feet of each other. She gave a nod and a slight cough, as instructed, to confirm that the Führer was in attendance. Alice saw the briefcase that he clutched with the remaining fingers of his single arm.

She returned to the kitchens and helped Frau Bender arrange berries in the shape of a swastika on the four cream cakes that would be brought in for dessert. This was a favorite dessert of the Führer's, and he loved the swastika on any dessert. The cake that the Führer was to be served had already had a slice taken by the taster, then reinserted and refrosted to cover the incisions. What if she could somehow lace a few of the berries on top of that slice with cyanide? So much easier than a bomb, and much less devastation.

She glanced at the clock and peered out the kitchen window. She saw that Wotan and his aide were now leaving the conference room. As planned, he had said he needed to freshen up. How long would it take for Wotan to put in the time pencil? Three minutes, five minutes, ten? He seemed so calm as he strode across the courtyard.

It took four minutes. He returned still clutching the briefcase.

"What's so interesting out the window?" Fräulein Wolk asked.

"Oh, nothing, just daydreaming. Lovely day. Clear blue skies." Alice sighed.

"You're missing a sweetheart at the front."

Alice blushed furiously. "Nooooo! Don't be ridiculous. I'm just thirteen. Not old enough to have a sweetheart, let alone one at the front."

She next saw a secretary from the communications room bustling across the courtyard. The call had come in! But she had to turn away from the window and just wait. Wotan and his aide should be leaving the conference room—without the briefcase. She fiddled with the berries on the cake, stared into the strawberry heart of the swastika.

"Oh, Ute, dear." Frau Bender called out. "I forgot to send over the Führer's digestive tablets. He takes them after the meal but before dessert. Would you be a dear and take them across to the center?" Alice felt her stomach drop. What could she do? The bomb would be going off in less than a minute and a half. The sweet paper had stated that four minutes after the call came in for Wotan, the bomb would explode. According to plan, Wotan had already left this innermost zone. A car was waiting. She would be blown to bits if she walked over there now.

"Ute? Did you hear me?"

"Yes, Frau Bender. I . . . I . . ." Should she walk fast or slow? Try to get there before the explosion and get back, or walk very slowly and hope she could miss being in the conference room when the bomb actually detonated?

"You what?" demanded Frau Bender.

"I am not feeling that well. I think I might need a digestive myself. I might throw up."

216

"Oh, nonsense. A big healthy girl like you!" She shoved the tablet bottle into Alice's hand. "Now on your way. Be quick about it."

Alice bent over and clutched her stomach. She walked slowly out the door. "Get on with it now!" Frau Bender called out through an open window in the kitchen as Alice stepped into the courtyard. She bent over more and made gagging noises.

In a split second, they were eclipsed by a thunderous clap. Shock waves seized the air. She was cast to the ground. A great cloud of soot erupted, filling the courtyard. Everything was shaking. In the kitchen, copper pots clanged to the floor. People stampeded from the conference center. Screams filled the air. A charred map of Russia floated out through what had been a window in the conference room and landed at Alice's feet, where she was curled up on the paving stones of the courtyard. She thought she glimpsed Hitler, supported by his high commander Wilhelm Keitel, leaning against a fragmented wall of the center.

He lives! Like a second explosion, the two words erupted in Alice's mind. She peeked out from where she lay on the ground and saw that there was a cut on the Führer's forehead, with blood leaking down over his stunned dark eyes. He appeared confused and momentarily deaf, as Keitel was screaming something in his ear. His pant leg was torn and bloody, but Adolf Hitler was standing. The Starling was still flying.

Alice tried to drag herself to her knees. But she collapsed again, and now she actually did vomit. *Well, at least I have an alibi,* she thought as she looked at her own puke on the paving stones. *I really was sick, Frau Bender. I told you so.*

For the next hour, all was chaos. She had no idea if Wotan had escaped. A plane was to be waiting for him to take him back to Berlin. She knew she must remain. Anyone who fled would immediately be suspected as a co-conspirator.

A few hours later, some maids who had stolen away from the Führer's private quarters returned giggling to the kitchen.

"You should have seen him!" Anya exclaimed to another who had been in his private quarters with the medical team. "He was absolutely elated. And showing off his wounds to Mussolini as his doctor treated him. 'I am immortal, invulnerable,' he kept saying."

Within another hour the compound was buzzing. There was one name on everyone's lips. "Stauffenberg!"

"He got through the checkpoints. . . . How he did, no one knows, but he did."

"The phone call was a ruse. The secretary who delivered the message for him to come for the call is a wreck. She's in much worse shape than the Führer."

By 6:30 that evening, Goebbels was on the radio confirming Hitler's survival and announcing that a violent attempt to overthrow the government had failed. And by midnight of that same evening, Stauffenberg, his aide, Haeften, and two others of the Valkyrie operation were led in front of a pile of sand in the courtyard of the Oberkommando der Wehrmacht, where they faced a ten-man firing squad. It was said that when the shots rang out, Stauffenberg shouted, "Long live holy Germany!"

TWENTY-FIVE

THE WINFIELDS CARRY ON

When she returned to Berlin three days later, Alice found her parents in a state of disbelief. Yet never for one second did they betray themselves. Still, there was a dimmed light in her father's eyes and a certain set to her mother's mouth. Nevertheless, the Winfields would carry on as they always had. Her parents had been through a lot in their lives, but never a war quite like this. Were they perhaps regretting having brought their youngest daughter into this? It only made her more resolute to carry on.

The Russians were advancing steadily from the east and had just delivered the biggest defeat to the German army. Hundreds of thousands of German troops were dead, wounded or missing. The Red Army was now closing in on Rumania.

But most frightening of all was that since the execution of Stauffenberg, thousands of other Germans had been charged as opponents of the Reich. And yet no one ever suspected the girl whose face none could remember, who had been in the target zone of the attempt, in a puddle of her own vomit.

Wotan was gone, but Alice was clearly expected to continue her work. A sweet paper had found its way to her within minutes of her arrival in Berlin. She had not even had to go to the drop spot to get it. Alice was told that her monitoring of the Führer's mental condition had become more vital than ever. She dutifully continued her work, spending a few days and nights every week in the Führerbunker, where new apartments had been added for the elite members of the Reich. The Goebbelses had moved in with their six children, and so had Göring and Bormann.

Alice's job was to help out at luncheon and dinner parties, and to be part of any performances—of which there were several. There were troops of Werewolf in the bunker now, including the handsome one, Fritz. He'd become quite the heartthrob of the young ladies who worked as secretaries or tasters in the Führerbunker. He was a flirtatious fellow. And he had a manner of tossing his head so that his silver-blond hair appeared to shimmer. Alice even caught Eva Braun tipping her head coquettishly when she spoke to him. Luckily the Führer seemed oblivious.

Thankfully, Alice was not of the age to interest him. Somehow, though, this made her think of Stefan Bacik, the Polish pilot who had first delivered her to her mission. Those burning green eyes! And the crinkly lines radiating out from them when he smiled. *Empathy.* That was the word that came to her when he smiled. The smile wasn't flirtatious at all, as with this fellow Fritz. It was something completely different. It said, "I want to understand you. You are someone of worth." She couldn't help but wonder if Stefan ever thought of her—wondered if she was dead or alive or, maybe worse, captured and sent to a concentration camp with the seven thousand others who had been rounded up after the assassination attempt.

School would not be starting until the fall, and during the day there was time to visit with David and resume her search for that face that had appeared in the crowd on the day she left for the Berghof.

David seemed better to her. He reported that the house was often empty except for the one servant, and he found it easy to pilfer food when no one was home. She wanted to tell David that she had seen Colonel Schmelling in the Führerbunker. But she couldn't tell him. It would lead to too many questions. Perhaps she could say something vague—to let him know that many of the highest officials were now residing in the Führerbunker. Even that seemed risky to Alice. It might make him too bold and lead him to take risks he shouldn't. For now he seemed okay at least—not fine, still painfully thin and he did cough a lot, but getting by.

222

He was nevertheless curious about Alice. But of course, he only knew her as Ute, and so she had to make up a whole fabricated history of herself. A very idyllic one. Summers in Norway, where her mother had relatives. Skiing in Kitz- bühel. In this scenario, her father was a businessman and her mother a secretary for a company that made glass. She had an older sister who had moved away and gotten married and now had a baby. It was when she said the word "baby," that tears welled in her eyes.

What would a baby of Louise's look like? Alice had just about given up on hunting for her sister. Although there was a difference of almost six years, she and Louise had shared a lot, a lot more than most sisters because of their peculiar situation, their destiny. And now Louise had rejected all that. Just thrown it all over, their history as a family, their rela- tionship as sisters.

Alice now realized that she had been angry all these months since Louise had her surgery. And then to top things off, Louise had changed the spelling of her name to Louisa— so pretentious. But Alice wasn't angry anymore. She was sad. Just plain sad.

"Ute?" David said. "Are you . . . about to cry?"

She blinked and felt a tear slide down her face. "Oh no . . . not really. I . . . I just feel bad that we haven't seen the baby in so long. All because of this stupid war."

"Your sister's baby?"

"Yes, that's the only one." She gave a sort of huff like a

223

chopped-off chuckle. "Maybe there'll be more." She paused. "If her husband returns."

"What's the baby's name?"

"Uh . . ." Should she make it a girl or boy? "Uh, it's Herman."

"I have an uncle Herman. We called him Hymie." David paused.

"Uh . . . I'm not sure . . . er . . . he's pretty young, so we just call him Herman for now."

"Herman for now is okay, just fine." He put out his hand and patted Alice's, as if to reassure her.

In that moment Alice knew two things: she knew that David knew she was lying, and she knew that she must find her sister in Berlin, no matter how long it took. She was convinced now that she had seen her.

TWENTY-SIX

A FLASH OF WHITE

A crisp autumnal wind blew a mixture of ashes and leaves on the sidewalk where Alice sat with her old school chums. Of course they had barely recognized her when they all returned to school ten days before. But then they finally remembered the RP girl who had done so well, they began pumping her with questions.

"So what does Eva Braun look like? I mean, gorgeous, of course, right?" Birgit asked.

"Well, not . . . not of course," Alice replied slowly. "She needs a lot of makeup. Her face is sort of . . . of . . ."

"Pasty?" Margret said almost hopefully.

"Not exactly pasty—kind of like tapioca pudding."

"Tapioca has bumps," the beautiful Lena offered. "If that's the case, I would suggest a salt mask. It draws imperfections to the surface."

"So you're suggesting I bring this up with the Führer's lady friend? Take a good look at this zit on my chin! It will be in full bloom by tomorrow."

The girls broke out laughing. They seemed to appreciate Alice's sense of humor. She made sure she wouldn't be seen as stuck-up, even though she got the highest marks.

And these girls were nice girls, even mousy Margret, who had ratlike tendencies. Yes, they believed all that Aryan pureness nonsense that Frau Mueller served up in their Racial Awareness class. But these beliefs were their Bible. It was their parents' Bible too. To question would make one a dissident or, worse, a Communist, or maybe a suspected Jew, and that would be fatal. It would invite terror into their lives. Now there was just plain old war.

At least twice a week, people had to take refuge in air-raid shelters from the bombs. They were being battered by both Russian and Allied troops. Let these girls wake up after the war. After their country had been defeated and humiliated worse than they ever had been before.

But once upon a time, Alice thought, *all of them must have started out in some way innocent.* Babies were born innocent. That's all babies were—just little packages of innocence. You could not be born a Nazi. You had to be taught and cultivated, like some rare seedling that would grow and bloom into a horrid flower. Alice pictured a rose, its blossoms opening. Then the rounded petals suddenly transforming into spikes.

Her mind began to wander back a winding cobbled lane in the Cotswolds, where they had once lived in a charming cottage. It was built of sandstone that softly glowed like gold, and scrambling up its walls were ribbons of roses and ivy. It was the loveliest place they had ever lived. Alice had called it the good witch cottage—as opposed to the bad witch cottage of Hansel and Gretel. It seemed like a fairy tale now, and here she was right smack in the land of the Brothers Grimm.

She heard her friends giggling. Their attention was focused on a table by the edge of the terrace where they sat.

"What's so funny?" Alice asked.

"Can't you see?" Birgit whispered. "Those two! They're necking!"

"Oh, oh!" She caught the flash of white. The two lovers had their backs to them, but their arms were entwined. The white hair sticking out from beneath the cap had to be Fritz, the Werewolf. The couple broke apart momentarily. The woman turned around.

Louise! Alice choked on her lemon fizz drink.

"Too much for you, Ute?" Margret laughed and poked her in the ribs. "My mother would kill me if I behaved like that in public."

Alice fought to stay calm. "Lucky for her you're not her mother," she answered glibly. *But my sister is necking with a Nazi Werewolf!* Louise had looked right at her and not even blinked. Her eyes were vacant. It was like the time Alice had walked home from school and run into Louise and two of

227

her friends in the village. Louise had looked straight at her, through her, without a flicker of recognition. Or the times in their very own house when Louise would startle as if Alice— or her own mother—was an intruder!

Now Alice was just another person at a café in Berlin. A faceless girl.

"You know, I'm running late. I better get going. I promised my mother I'd try for some real bread at that bakery on Hoffmannstrasse."

"Good luck," Lena said.

Alice was already getting up. She noticed that Louise—or was it Louisa?—had hung her pocketbook on the back of her chair. She quickly swept by the table. The scent was there— Laurel Bright. It swirled around Alice's head. But she had never been more alert. She stumbled a bit on purpose, knocking the pocketbook off the chair. She stooped to pick it up.

"Oh, pardon me, Fräulein. I'm so clumsy."

Louise bent over to retrieve it at the same time. "Not to worry." Their faces were mere inches apart. The scent flooded the space between them. "Lovely perfume," Alice murmured.

And still not even a twinkle of recognition. In fact, it felt as if in that moment the entire world had gone dark.

TWENTY-SEVEN

ALICE I AM

"You're not yourself," Posie Winfield said to Alice upon her return from the fateful afternoon at the café. *And what self would that be?* Alice thought. But she said nothing.

Now five days had passed since she had stopped to pick up that pocketbook of her sister's and their eyes had locked. Her sister's eyes, totally blank. *All right,* Alice had thought. *If this is how you want to play it, I'll go along.*

Alice had waited at a corner behind a newsstand just outside her sister's line of vision until the pair got up to leave. They walked off arm in arm. Alice followed. The couple parted ways after a lingering kiss. Alice thought she'd throw up. She followed Louise for the better part of an hour until Louise entered an apartment building. Alice waited as long as she could, hoping Louise would leave the building again.

But she didn't. Alice was back the next day before school to see if she could catch her leaving the building. No luck. But she was patient. A cardinal rule of spycraft.

Alice was obsessed, yet at the same time she was worried about David. It was as if two thoughts were warring in her head. Louise and David. His cough had worsened. Autumn had turned damp and chilly. Winter was knocking at the door, and the Russians were breathing down Berlin's neck. American B-17s had begun bombing the city again. So the Winfields were still in their basement apartment, and Alan Winfield had started to work on an exit plan. But what about David? Alice would often come home and find her father poring over maps. "They're close to the Vistula River. They cross that and Berlin is done for," he murmured.

"They? The Russians? The Red Army?"

"Who else?" He looked up and smiled. "Their artillery divisions. They only need to be six, seven miles away to shell us. The Reds and their rocket launchers—Stalin's organ, they call the launchers."

"Who calls them that?" Alice asked.

"The Germans. The rocket makes a howling sound that is absolutely terrifying. I hope we're out of here by the time they come."

"But how, Papa? How will we get out?"

"I'm working on it. I'm working. Be patient."

In that moment, she was so tempted to tell him that she had seen Louise. But she couldn't. She hesitated to say anything before she confronted Louise herself. Was Louise some kind of double agent? Why was she here? Here in Berlin with her new face?

Twice she had waited for Louise outside her building, but she had never gotten up her nerve to actually confront her again. She couldn't bear to have Louise look through her again. The nothingness in those eyes, the absolute void, was excruciating. Alice felt it was as if she had endured an amputation of sorts, as if a limb had been severed. She had to think of something else.

But at the same time, she knew she should go visit David. He needed something for his cough. She had bought some sort of disgusting tonic the other day but had become so obsessed with her thoughts of Louise that she had actually forgotten to go see him. She would go now.

"Going out?" said her mother when she had retrieved the cough syrup and tucked it into her jacket.

"Yeah, just for a little bit. I said I'd help Lena with some homework."

Lying, she thought. *It comes so easy now that I'm a spy.* But if her parents knew that she was protecting a little Jewish boy in hiding, they would be out of their minds with fear— fear that their covers would be compromised. They would all be endangered. There were simply too many risks involved in telling her parents. And she remembered something that Louise had told her when she had decided to leave the Rasa service and have her surgery. *I've grown tired of it. I was always living this lie.* Then Louise had said the thing about the cute Norwegian guy who was trying to woo her. *What could I tell him? This isn't really me?*

But this new Louise didn't even recognize her own sister. *Well,* Alice thought, *she had to push that out of her mind.* She had to go over to the whipped-cream house and see David. David, who never seemed to forget her face. The thought still startled her. David indeed never ever forgot her face. He always seemed to recognize her. How very odd. Was it because he led such a solitary life, always in hiding? His world had shrunk to the hidden cubbyhole in the cellar of his house, the alley, and the trees. And she was the only person in that little world.

Usually David perched up in a tree during the daylight hours. Together they had constructed a little platform in his favorite tree. It was more visible now as autumn progressed and the leaves began to fall. Maybe things were too visible, as she now heard a cough from behind a pile of rubbish. She walked over.

"David?"

"Good evening." He coughed again. "Well, not quite evening, I guess, though the days are getting shorter."

"David, what are you doing here? Why . . . why aren't you in the tree? Yes, it's daytime, but still."

"Don't worry. The leaves are dropping and . . . and . . ." His voice, which was very thin and gaspy, dropped off. "I was just too tired, Ute."

"David, it will be November soon and it's cold and you

don't sound good. You need to be inside somewhere."

"They've moved back in temporarily, I think. The Schmellings." He nodded toward the house.

Alice felt a panic rising in her like a fast incoming tide. She was almost gasping herself. David looked feverish, and his eyes were glazed and almost too shiny. This was dangerous.

"Here, I brought you some cough syrup." She took out the bottle, unscrewed the cap, and held it out. He didn't reach for it.

"Can you help me?"

"Oh . . . oh, sure. Of course." She put one arm around his back and lifted him; then, supporting him, she tipped the bottle to his mouth. He scrunched up his face and gave her a kind of half smile. "Worse it tastes, the better it works. That's what my father always said about medicine."

"I hope he's right." Alice was thinking that she had to do something and do it fast. She wished she could bring him back to the garage, but there was no way. If they were discovered harboring a Jew in the Reich garage, the game would be up. But what about Louise? She lived in that rather nice apartment building. Couldn't she tuck away one very ill child? But what if Fritz was there? *Oh God,* thought Alice. Panic was engulfing her.

First things first, her mum always said. She had to find something warm for him. She needed to get a blanket or something. She couldn't go home and take one of theirs. Her mother would immediately become suspicious—but what about the Führerbunker? Her own little cubbyhole of a room.

She could surely sneak out one of the comforters from her bed. She also remembered that she kept a warm jacket there.

"David, you stay right here," she said, peeling off her own jacket.

"You think I'm going somewhere?" He laughed but began coughing again. He wiped his mouth with his sleeve. She saw blood streaks.

"I'm going to get you something warm to sleep under. It won't take me long."

"Ute?"

"Yes?"

"Ute, we don't know much about each other . . . but do you think you could take me home with you?"

She felt as if her heart dropped out of her body. The seconds dripped by, and a silence filled the air between them. And then a maverick breeze blew through the alley and erased the quiet. All she could hear now was her own heart beating, beating, clamped around its dark and very dangerous secret.

Her voice was guttural as she spoke. "David, my name is not Ute. It is Alice. And I'm a spy."

"Alice," he said softly. "I love your name, Alice. I love saying it. It's . . . it's delicious."

"And what does it taste like, David?"

"Like lingonberry jam on buttered toast."

TWENTY-EIGHT
"YOU'LL HAVE TO KILL ME, WON'T YOU?"

Her backpack was stuffed with a warm eiderdown comforter, in addition to a jacket and a sweater she'd taken from her minuscule room at the Führerbunker, and a thermos of hot chocolate she had filled from the pot in the staff kitchen. She began racing back to the alley. She was taking a shortcut when a figure emerged from a narrow street called Kleine Gasse, which meant small alley.

It was a woman. She was rushing, and her back was toward Alice. But there was something about the set of her shoulders . . . Alice knew without a doubt that it was Louise. Her face might have changed, but her shoulders, the way she was walking, had not.

"Louise!" Alice called out. There was not even a hitch in the woman's gait. Not a flinch in her shoulders. She merely walked on. Alice sprang toward her and struck her on the shoulder. "You!"

Louise turned around, but her face was completely placid.

"Yes?" She opened her wide gray eyes. Those hadn't changed.

"Louise, or sorry, Louisa, it's me, Alice . . . your sister." She whispered this in English.

"I'm afraid I don't speak English," the woman replied in German—German with an Alsatian accent.

"Are you going to deny this?" Alice continued in English.

"I don't know what you are talking about, little girl," Louise answered in German. "Now I am in a hurry."

"I bet you are," Alice hissed as Louise rushed ahead. "What are you? You can't be a spy for them!"

The woman turned. Her face seemed to have changed. It was filled with a new kind of anger—an anger that Alice had never seen on her old face or this new one.

"And if I am?" she asked, still in German.

"You'll have to kill me, won't you?" Alice replied.

"Or you me?"

Alice felt as if she had been punched. As if all the wind had been knocked out of her. She was almost surprised to find herself still standing. She took a few tentative steps, but she was shaking so hard she felt she might fall down. She tried to steady her breathing. She leaned up against a wall at the corner of the street where the skeleton of a bombed-out building stood. She looked at the jagged remains. She felt as if she was a ruin herself—the ruin of a creature who had once been a sister. The world suddenly seemed empty to her. Slowly she crumpled to the ground.

"Oh my god, my god," she whispered to the pavement. "My god . . . my god . . ."

She stared at the place where she and Louise had stood glaring at each other. There was no sign of Louise, not even the sound of her high-heeled shoes on the pavement as she walked away. She had simply vanished.

Alice was uncertain how long she remained on her knees, but finally the weight on her back, the backpack stuffed with warm things, reminded her. David was out here. David needed her. He needed the blankets, the sweater, the hot chocolate. Slowly she got to her feet and walked on.

David peered out from the voluminous cloud of blankets she had wrapped him in. She held the thermos cup to his mouth.

"So tell me more about this . . . this group, the Rasa. You said they started during the time of Henry VIII."

"Yes, it was the king's spymaster, William Morfitt. It's kind of a long story. I'll try to make it short."

"Don't worry. I don't have much to do. I have all the time in the world," David replied with a wan smile.

"Well, it really started around the time of the Field of the Cloth of Gold. Do you know about that?"

"Yes, a bit. Henry VIII met with the French king."

"Francis I, near Calais. Sir William had been inserted as

a spy. Unfortunately, he was caught and thrown in prison. A woman came into the prison. The way the story is told, she was a French peasant woman. She carried a basket full of mushrooms. She told William Morfitt that he must follow her. There was no moon, a very dark night, one she explained was called the Lune des Champignons. Which basically meant no moon at all except for the pale gray mushrooms, champignons, on the ground. Some said they resembled little moons. Instead of walking toward the forest where the mushrooms might grow, the woman led William to the beach, where a boat was waiting. And he escaped.

"The entire way back, he tried to remember the woman's face, but he simply couldn't. It was as if it was erased like chalk on a blackboard. Then he recalled that a few months before, he had received some information concerning the Pope—not the king's favorite."

David gave a short little chuckle. This encouraged Alice. He seemed to be feeling better. "So Morfitt tried to track down the source of this information. For some reason he thought he might have been from Scotland. But he could not seem to place his face. It bedeviled him for days. How could the face of someone who had brought such pressing intelligence to the court of Henry VIII be so forgettable?

"He remembered this as he sailed back from France— twice within a very short time, someone had aided him, and yet he could not keep their faces in his mind. How odd! As a spy, he prided himself on his memory. It was vital to his duties. Due to the fact that these two incidents occurred in such close proximity in terms of time, those faces, or non-faces, began to haunt him. He began to imagine how effective it would be if there was an intelligence operation, a network of spies whose faces no one could remember. They would be virtually faceless.

"Eventually he found that original spy who had come with the information concerning the Pope. We call him Rob in Rasa history. Rob led William Morfitt to others who shared his condition. Most of them were thieves, and often grave robbers charging doctors high prices for the bodies they retrieved for medical studies. The thieves were rarely caught, and when they were, they proved to be masters in the art of escape.

"Within just two years and with His Majesty's blessing, Sir William—for he had been knighted by this time—had created a new secret intelligence agency, the most adept in the world. They were called Rasas for 'tabula rasa,' since the memory of their faces was always erased. Thus far, the Rasas have endured for almost four hundred years. So that's my story, our story."

"Not for everyone," David said.

"Not for everyone . . . what?"

"Your face was not erased for me. Not at all. I remember everything about you, since the first day we met, up there." He pointed to the bare tree limbs above where they were now crouching.

"I guess not. But believe me, you're the exception."

"But you said that this was your first mission."

"True, but you know my mum and dad were often on missions where I would go with them. We've had to move around quite a bit—new schools, all of that. It took people a long time to remember me every time I started a new school."

"But now you are on a mission, with your parents here in Berlin."

She hesitated a moment. She should not be telling David any of this. But he was her best friend. Friends told the truth. Friends confided in each other. And right now, she felt she had nothing else to lose but a best friend.

"We each have different tasks. Mum works at the OKH—the High Command of the General Army, with an attachment to the Oberkommando der Wehrmacht, another branch of the army. A lot of information flows through there. And my father is in the Reich garage, where all the official ministry cars are serviced."

"And you are an RP and get to be right in the thick of it with the man himself!"

"Indeed."

"Does he remember you?"

"Not exactly. He sometimes asks for the RP girl who plays one of the Valkyries. He seems to recall me only when I'm in full dress—cape, shield, a helmet, and wings on top. The whole rigamarole."

David laughed softly, which seemed to trigger a hacking

coughing fit. He pressed the edge of the blanket to his mouth. Alice looked away. She knew there would be bloodstains.

"I'm really okay, Alice. Especially since you brought all this warm stuff. I'm not nearly as cold anymore."

"All right, but I'll be back tomorrow with more warm clothes, and I'm going to look for that medicine you told me about and see if I can find any at home. But in the meantime, I think you should sleep in that empty trash bin. We can turn it on its side, and I can help stuff you in there with all your blankets. It might rain tonight, or even snow. You'll be protected."

David agreed. It took a few minutes as she carefully placed one blanket on the bottom. Then David crawled in, and she carefully folded the other blankets on top of him, tucking them tightly around his frail body.

Alice prayed he would stay warm.

She prayed it would not snow or rain.

She didn't pray for her sister. Her sister was gone. As good as dead. Praying for the dead always seemed stupid to Alice.

As she got up to leave, David whispered in his hoarse voice. "Good night, Alice."

TWENTY-NINE

NOBODY CHARLESTONS LIKE LOUISE

"I don't approve, no, not at all!" Frau Weissmann made a tsking sound as Alice entered the Führerbunker. "Those parties at the chancellery are becoming very . . . very . . ." She seemed to be searching for a word.

"Risqué?" Alice offered. Risqué was her mother's favorite word for indecent displays.

"Uh, worse . . . bawdy. Dancing ladies and drunkenness."

"So why do I have to go?" She had left David earlier to get some medicine, but a message had come through to the garage that her presence was required at the Führerbunker. "Rats!" she muttered, but tucked the bottle of cough syrup into a pocket and headed toward the Führerbunker. She would have to go to David later.

As she stepped into the kitchen to find Frau Weissmann,

she saw the woman hovering over a platter of hors d'oeuvres.

"Oh, thank goodness you came." Frau Weissmann looked up. "The Führer's secretary says there is talk about a performance here in the bunker tonight. So I put your costume out for you, but first, can you go over there, to the grand reception room? They need extra help for passing food, and I just made up two more trays of the little sandwiches."

"I've never served before in the chancellery. It's much more formal than the Berghof. What do I do?"

"Not formal anymore, with questionable women prancing about. There's nothing to serving. Just go up with the tray and say, 'Pardon me, would you like a canapé?'" She giggled. "And then you can say, 'Please keep your cleavage out of the caviar.'"

"All right." Alice laughed. She couldn't help but think that in many ways there was more to Frau Weissmann than met the eye.

But why did she have to serve tonight, of all nights? David seemed so ill. This morning she was sure he had been running a fever. She wanted to get back one more time before it was dark. Nevertheless, she returned to her quarters and dressed in her uniform. Her white apron was a little less than crisp.

"Shouldn't I iron this apron?" she asked as Frau Weissmann handed her the tray.

"No, never mind! They're in a hurry. The people have already started arriving—early!"

Was this a sign that they were getting desperate? The war had started to enter a new and critical phase. Things had not been going well since July, when the Red Army had established bridgeheads on the Vistula River. They were pushing, and pushing fast, toward Warsaw, and after Warsaw it would be a hop, skip, and a jump to Vienna, and after Vienna . . . well, no one wanted to think about it.

A sort of manic frivolity was beginning to build, in indirect proportion to the decline of the German front. On October 21, the Red Army had taken Nemmersdorf, a German city in East Prussia that was not far from the Wolf's Lair. It had been a massacre as the Russian slaughtered their way westward. So what else would one do in the face of a massacre but throw a party?

Alice stood in the arched entrance to the grand reception room with her platter of canapés and observed the manic festivities. It was more than unbelievable. It was fantastically incredible as she watched people throwing back their heads, gulping glass after glass of champagne. A flash of white, and she quickly spied Fritz, who had dispensed entirely with his glass and was swigging directly from a bottle as he pointed to something at the center of a clot of people. At the edges of the crowd, a man was playing the trombone. Alice recognized it—

It was the music for the Charleston.

With her platter of sandwiches, Alice edged toward the fringes of the crowd. She was within inches of Fritz's elbow.

He turned to get a canapé, and handed the bottle of champagne to the fellow next to him.

"Isn't she a marvel?" he exclaimed. "Look at her! Just look. No one Charlestons like Helga."

Yes, thought Alice, *no one does Charleston like Helga . . . except for Louise.* And it was Louise who was doing the manic fast step, kicking her feet, both forward and backward, swinging her arms and tossing her head back with gales of laughter.

Alice turned to a man with a silvery handlebar mustache. "Here, sir." The man was startled as she handed him her platter and dashed out into the circle and began dancing side by side with her sister, who did not blink an eye. Alice knew all the steps—the Shorty George, where you kept your knees almost touching and stepped forward on the balls of your feet. Spank the Baby, where you slid forward with one foot, slapping your butt with your opposite hand. Apple Jacks, with knee slaps and cross touches. You name it, the sisters had it down pat.

Soon the people were cheering, "More, more . . . those girls can dance!" They had been dancing for three or four minutes. Smiling at each other, kicking forward toward each other until they were just a foot away and slapping each other's hands in the cross touches. Then stepping back and doing the knee knocks where they would crouch down side by side, each knocking her knees together and then crossing her hands. Idiotic looking but oh so fun!

But did Louise ever betray even a glimmer of recognition? Never!

But there was one person who did seem to have a trace of dim recollection. The Führer had stepped up to the edge of the circle. His eyes were fastened on Alice. He tipped his head toward his minister of propaganda, Joseph Goebbels. Alice felt their eyes on her now. A dread began building in the pit of her stomach. He had never recognized her before, except for that night in the kitchen at the Berghof. But she had been wearing her Valkyrie braids then, certainly a memory prompt. Maybe he was recalling that night in the kitchen and not really seeing her but the Valkyrie Brünnhilde, that he had imagined her to be in the kitchen that night as she cut the apple cake. The Führer cake.

Fragments of the kitchen conversation came back to her. The Führer had said, *Mit den Zöpfen . . . . Brünnhilde! You have come to save me, you dear child. Dear Brünnhilde has come to save me with some apple cake.* She could not let him observe her a second longer. "Bye-bye, Helga! It's been fun." Alice shimmied away from the center of the circle and retrieved the platter of canapés.

Five minutes later she was back in the Führerbunker.

"I'm afraid I have to go home, Frau Weissmann. I'm not feeling well at all. I think I might be coming down with something. I wouldn't want to infect our dear Führer."

"Of course not, dearie. You probably just got sick watching those goings-on." As she frowned, the lines in her face suddenly collided. "You run along. Would you like me to fix up a thermos of beef broth? I have some on the stove right now."

"Oh, that would be lovely, yes, please do." When she had raced out of the chancellery to the bunker, a shroud of snow had been falling on the city, and all she could think of was David. Beef broth and more warm clothes would be perfect. She would go straight to the whipped-cream house. He'd been good about sleeping in the trash can. She hoped he was there tonight.

The swollen moon was just a smear behind the scrim of snow that began to fall more heavily as she raced toward the alley. There seemed to be no separation between the skin of the earth and the grayness of the starless sky.

THIRTY

WINTER BLOOM

She turned into the alley and ran through the nearly blinding snow toward the overturned trash bin.

"David!" she whispered as she approached. But there was no answer. No cough. Indeed, there seemed to be an odd hollowness that greeted her. She stopped a few feet away. She knew before she looked into it that the bin would be empty. There was not even a blanket, nor the old thermos she had brought with hot chocolate.

"David!" she called louder. There was still no answer. Where could he have gone? He wasn't strong enough to walk a block, let alone climb a tree. She stood completely bewildered in the alley.

The snow collected in her collar. She could feel the heat of the thermos in her backpack. She felt a panic rising within her. Where could he be? Had he gone back into the house? But he had told her it was dangerous now, and the window well had been closed up tight with a thick board. He wasn't sure why.

She looked around. She called softly again. She had to do something. She walked along the back wall that continued the length of the alley. Two houses down from David's house, she found one alley door that was open to someone's garden. She walked through. The hedges that separated the back gardens of the neighboring house were covered in mantles of thick snow. But she could see that the hedge directly ahead had been broken through. Not only broken through, but as she approached, she saw that there was a tuft of eiderdown. She reached out and took it. This was not from a duck that had flown over the garden, but from the quilt she had brought David. She was sure.

She pushed through the hedge. Then she saw the shallow depressions, like shadows in the snow. He had walked this way. It must be David. The snow was falling so fast that the shoe prints were being erased quickly. But there was a crust of bread. She bent over to pick it up. It was from the bread she had brought him before. She had been bringing him food whenever she could.

Within a few steps, she stopped short. There were clear footprints with dark spots in the snow. She crouched down—blood! She felt a strange paralysis seize her. Eider fluff, bread crumbs, and blood! This was like a darker Hansel and Gretel story. Where would it lead? She heard a soft cough and raced across the next yard and through the hedge.

She was in the secret garden again. The moon suddenly rolled out from behind the thick clouds and showered silver light on the snow. It was magical. She saw him beneath the branch of the alley tree they had once perched in when he had first shown her the secret garden. Alice called his name softly as she approached. But there was nothing. "David!" she shouted, then screamed. She rushed toward him. Leaning against the tree, David Bloom looked like a collapsed marionette. The quilt had fallen away, as had the blankets. She reached out for him and now whispered, "David, David . . . no . . . no . . . no . . ."

She noticed a small piece of paper in his lap. She picked it up. There was writing on it. But through her tears she could hardly read it. Then, gasping and gulping, she wiped her eyes, and the writing became visible.

> *Thank you, Alice.*
> *I came to see the hellebore—winter bloom, you know. See it right over there by the birch tree?*
> *Love,*
> *David*

She covered her mouth and moaned. Then, sobbing, she folded his frail body into her arms, and began to rock back and forth.

* * *

She would leave him here in his mother's secret garden. For this was where their souls might meet. She would leave him and cover him in snow. When she was finished, she walked over and broke off some of the branches from the weeping pines—the rabbis, as David called them—and placed them over the snowy mound. She settled down at the base of the birch tree and cried and cried and cried, until the first streaks of the dawn and the morning star began to rise in the east.

The words of the Kaddish, the Hebrew Mourner's prayer that she had learned in Rasa camp came back to her quickly, and she began to whisper these words into the soft breeze.

May His great name be exalted and sanctified. In the world which He created according to His will! May He establish His kingdom during your lifetime and during your days and during the lifetimes of all the House of Israel, speedily and very soon! And say, Amen. May His great name be blessed for ever, and to all eternity!

THIRTY-ONE

WOULD SHE RATHER?

What happened on that late November night in the snow-swathed garden would be her secret. Alice Winfield would never tell anyone about David. She found herself often thinking about him with a profound sadness. He remembered her. He never forgot her name, Ute, but how delighted he had been when she told him her real name, Alice. She recalled that time, just a day before, when she had told him that she was a spy and her name was not Ute but Alice. *I love your name, Alice. I love saying it. It's . . . it's delicious.* She had laughed and asked what her name tasted like? Without hesitating, he had answered, *Like lingonberry jam on buttered toast.*

But she tried as best she could to push such memories out of her mind. Things were becoming too dangerous. Hitler had left Berlin soon after the party at the Reich Chancellery. He had headed first to the Wolf's Lair, and then, on December 10, in his special train to the Eagle's Nest, a secret camouflaged complex in the woods near Berchtesgaden.

She was not required to attend, as the Christmas holidays were approaching. Not that there was much to celebrate. The air raids had multiplied. Alice and her family lived almost exclusively in the basement of the Reich garage. If they happened to be out, they often had to run to the nearest air-raid shelter. It was hardly a festive season. According to her mother, the people in the OKH office were stupefied by Hitler's complete denial of the facts that were surging into the ministry's office. From the Baltic Sea to the Adriatic, nearly seven million Russian troops had massed in a hard line, and yet Hitler didn't believe it. The German intelligence reports were "completely idiotic," according to Hitler.

Nevertheless, the rest of the city was hardly in the mood to celebrate the holidays. There would be no Christmas goose, for there were no geese, ducks, or even chickens.

Every citizen was on short rations. And the people became gaunt. Children's eyes grew larger and ringed in shadows as their bodies shrank around their bones. There was no "Stille Nacht"—"Silent Night"—to be sung. What humor was left turned dark. A favorite joke in the season of merriment was that, as a Christmas gift, "one should be practical and give a coffin."

Because of the frequent air raids, Alice's school was let out early for the holidays and no return date was set. When walking by a house not that far from David's, Alice saw that one had been reduced to only two standing walls. Scrawled on the brick was a message: "Erich, we are fine. We are staying with the Obers." Alice surmised that Erich was a soldier returning from the front.

The air raids increased. There was a pattern, with the British bombing by day and the Americans at night. The Red Army was expected to surround Budapest by Christmas Eve. In another favorite joke, the initials LSR, which stood for Luftschutzraum, or air-raid shelter, were said to mean "Learn Russian quickly."

On Christmas Eve the Winfields sat down to a strange dish made of tinned liverwurst that Posie had mashed into patties and cooked with mutton fat and chopped onion. They smeared it on disgusting bread made from pea meal flour and barley.

Alice looked at the gray mess on her plate. "I am almost longing for snoek." She sighed.

Her mother laughed and reached over and patted her hand. Then she got up and turned the sound loud on the gramophone. How many times had Alice listened to the four operas of the Ring cycle? One hundred? She knew every word. Every note. These days in their apartment at the garage, the Winfields always had the gramophone playing to camouflage their conversation. They were focused on leaving Berlin as soon as they could.

There was an essential irony to their situation. Alan Winfield, or rather Gunther Schnaubel, was the director of

254

motor vehicle operations in the Bendlerstrasse garage of the war department. He had dozens of automobiles at his disposal. So why not just drive out of Berlin and head toward the Elbe River, at most a two-and-a-half-hour drive from where they were?

There was a petrol shortage, for one thing. And secondly, these automobiles were all designated for the highest-ranking members of the Nazi party. With Alice's father as chauffeur, were Posie and Alice supposed to be Magda Goebbels and one of her daughters? Or Maybe Frau Bormann and one of her ten children? Could they pretend to be staff for one of those men? Alice was too young to pass for a secretary.

They went through every possibility and permutation, including one where her father wore a chauffeur's uniform. They had even toyed with the idea of Alice and Posie hiding in the trunk, but there were simply too many checkpoints where they could be discovered.

"I could possibly find an old wreck of an automobile. Fix it up with no insignias and we could . . ." Alan Winfield's voice began to dwindle.

"Could what, dear? Pretend we're going on a picnic?" Posie said, getting up and turning the music louder. This was how their conversations went, in fits and starts, then quick whispered exchanges in an indecipherable Rasa code that was often composed of poems. Alan slowly began to recite one of the poems now.

"All quiet, said the star rising in the east . . . until the dawn break sea when the waves do curl and hurl their force upon

255

this gaunt and hollow land."

Both Alice's and Posie's eyes opened wide. Posie tipped her head and indicated that Alice should fetch a piece of paper and pen to write with. She came back.

"Oh, Papa, what a lovely poem. Can you say it again?"

"There's probably more. That's just one short verse . . . but I can't remember it all, dear child." This too was code. Which meant, invert the third and sixth words of each sentence and apply the grid. The Morfitt grid was a basic decoding grid that could be applied to encrypted messages.

Within ten minutes Alice and her mother knew what their father was suggesting. They must be patient until the roads were clear of snow, then get bicycles. With any luck they could get to the Elbe in two and a half days.

"Two and a half days! I'm not that old, dear," Posie exclaimed. "Two days, tops."

"Weather permitting." Alan grinned at his wife. "We can take the underground from Alexanderplatz, if it hasn't been bombed by then."

"But where do we get the bikes?" They had turned the music even louder.

"I have some ideas. But keep your eyes open for wrecked ones. I can fix them up in no time. That I can assure you."

There was a knock on the door. The three Winfields exchanged glances.

"Who could that be on Christmas Eve?" Posie asked as she got up. "Coming!" she cried out.

Alice had a fleeting thought. She caught her breath. Could it be Louise? A kind of Christmas miracle? Their family made whole again! Of course she had never mentioned to her parents that she had spotted Louise three times. She wasn't sure if they would believe her. And then there was the lingering doubt that Louise could be a spy for the Nazis. The dreadful words they had exchanged in the alley came back to her.

What are you? You can't be a spy for them!

And if I am?

You'll have to kill me, won't you?

Or you me?

But how could she bear to be snuggling up and kissing that horrid Werewolf Fritz? Louise had not really had that many boyfriends. Just a few in Rasa camp when she was younger, and the fellow in Norway, but he couldn't ever remember her. But Fritz was unimaginable, with those cruel sky-blue Nazi eyes. No, it was absolutely inconceivable to Alice that her sister had kissed that man. She couldn't bear to think of it.

"Walter!" Alice's mother exclaimed. "What brings you out on Christmas Eve?"

"Oh, I wouldn't have interrupted, but a message came through." He took a deep breath that seemed almost painful for him.

"Please come in and sit down. I'll get you some schnapps."

"Not necessary."

"The Red Army has almost surrounded Budapest. I am to

257

inform the director that both Goebbels's auto and Himmler's need to be made ready."

Alice's father was standing up now. "Yes, of course."

"I shall be happy to stay on and help you. I believe there were some fuel injector issues with one and then some idling problems with the other."

"The fuel injector issues were with the late Colonel Stauffenberg's auto. Both Himmler's and Goebbels's have problems with idling when letting up on the throttle. You need not stay. I can take care of this."

"If you need me, sir, I can stay."

"No, you need to go home to that young wife of yours."

Walter turned gray. "I am afraid, sir, that my wife died last night."

"What?" Alan said in dismay, and Posie emitted a little shriek.

"We were caught out during that raid. We went to the nearest shelter over on Potsdamer Platz. Bad air, you know. So we moved up to the next level. But my wife had been sitting on the floor. She got too much of it and fainted and . . . and then I carried her up to a higher level in the shelter, but she was dead by the time I got her there."

"Oh . . . oh my goodness, Walter!" Posie gasped.

"Would you like to stay here? We can fix something up for you."

"No, Frau Schnaubel. I really must go and look after my mother and grandmother."

"Yes, of course," Posie said. Alan Winfield came over and

258

gave the young man a pat on the shoulder.

Just before he walked out the door, Walter turned. "What does it all mean, Herr Schnaubel? What does it all mean?"

"It means, for one thing, that we are losing this war, and that the Führer is deluding himself."

"Herr Director Schnaubel," Walter said in a tremulous voice. "That is a dangerous thing to say, is it not?"

"It's the truth. But lies are even more dangerous. There are eight thousand Russian airplanes concentrated on the Vistula River and the East Prussian front. Göring has convinced the Führer that they are decoy airplanes, dummy ones, just to frighten the Germans. And the Führer believes him. That, son, is dangerous."

"Ja, Herr Schnaubel, I heard the same. The planes aren't dummies. But now I have nothing to lose." He walked out and shut the door behind him.

When Alice went to bed that night, she thought about Walter. Walter and his dead wife. And then she thought of Louise. Louise and Fritz. She couldn't bear it.

1945,

BERLIN, GERMANY

THIRTY-TWO

MORE FIDDLING

Things began to move very quickly. On January 12, 1945, the offensive began. It began at five in the morning, but word did not come through to Berlin until later that day. Less than twenty-four hours later, on the morning of January 13, the attack on East Prussia began, scant miles from the Wolf's Lair. On January 16, Hitler moved into the Berlin Führerbunker permanently.

But, of course, words like "permanent" were not spoken. It was rumored that his top aides, including Bormann and Göring, urged Hitler to go to the Berghof. Nevertheless, a message was delivered to the garage that a Ring cycle performance was planned, and Ute's presence might soon be required.

"Mein Gott!" Alan Winfield slapped his forehead in dismay as the messenger left. "This is crazy!"

"I don't want her to go, dear."

"No, no. She should go. She'll be safer there in the Führerbunker when they start to bomb."

"How are the bikes coming?" Posie asked.

"I've rescued five wrecked ones. Between five, I think I can get at least three new ones out of their parts."

"Well, if you can't do it, nobody can."

"With half a meter of snow on the ground, we're not going to get far. We'll have to wait until it melts and the roads are passable."

"So they called you back!" Frau Weissmann was obviously upset. "Simply ridiculous!"

"What is ridiculous, Frau Weissmann?"

"The city is doomed, and what is the biggest tempest in the Führerbunker teapot?"

"What is it, Frau Weissmann?"

"It seems that the Führer wants his collection of original scores of the operas, which Wagner's son had given him, transferred to the bunker. Winifred Wagner is objecting, and so is her son, Wieland Wagner, the director. Imagine arguing about such things at a time like this!"

"Yes, I see what you mean."

"I knew you would, you're such a smart girl." She sighed. "Your costume is ready, of course."

"And when is the performance?"

"I don't know."

"Do you know which scenes?"

"I'm not sure, but those fellows are being brought in to install the scenery."

"What fellows?"

"Oh, you know. The wolfies."

"The Werewolf. Yes, I saw a lot of them in the courtyard when I arrived."

"Well, you know the way to your quarters. I'm sure there'll be a rehearsal called soon."

"Who else is playing the roles?"

"Let's see, Marta from the pastry kitchen, as well as Gerda or Margot, one of the tasters. I get them mixed up." She shook her head and made a soft clicking sound of disapproval. "What a terrible job they have. And yes, some of the Goebbels children. The entire Goebbels family has moved in with all their furniture, so it seems." She sighed. "I wish I could remember which of the operas it is." She tapped her head as if trying to jostle her brain just a bit. "Oh! I believe it's the last one of the four, *Götterdämmerung*."

"Oh!" Alice exclaimed softly. *The Twilight of the Gods.* The collapse of all things. For that was the translation. *Seems appropriate,* she thought. However, they had never staged that one before. Of course it was the one where the Valkyrie Brünnhilde rides her horse into the flames of the funeral pyre of Siegfried, the lover who betrayed her. But Alice had never played the role of this last act. She had to admit it gave her a slightly queasy feeling.

Ten minutes later, she felt more than just slightly queasy as she turned a corner in the labyrinthine passageways of the Führerbunker and nearly bumped into Fritz.

"Ooop! Pardon me," he said quickly. And then said, "Wait a minute! Don't I know you somehow?"

"No, no. I don't believe so."

He tipped his head slightly to the side and studied her. Her heart was racing. "Weren't . . . you . . . the . . . the dancing girl?"

"I . . . I don't dance."

"Oh, sorry. Maybe I'm wrong." He turned and walked off.

Alice felt as if she had been punched in the stomach. She stopped and leaned against the wall. How could he have recognized her? This had never happened before. Then a very disturbing thought slithered into her mind. The only person who had always known her face and never forgot it was David. She hated to think that this evil person, this Werewolf, shared anything with David.

For the next two weeks she wrestled with telling someone. But she was not sure who. She didn't want to tell her parents about this. It would worry them too much. Berlin was full of spies. MI6 ones, and those from other British agencies like the Special Operations Executive. Her primary fios, Stauffenberg, was gone. But dead drop contacts must still be around. She never really knew who they were. She'd just leave the chalk mark, then leave the coded message at the dead drop site. It was always tempting to hang around and see who the person was who picked it up, but she knew it was risky. She should never do it. In an emergency, she could get a message to him—a crust of bread, an apple peel—and set up a meeting. It only took her a split second to decide that in fact this was an emergency. She could be in grave danger with Fritz almost but not quite recognizing her.

There was a new dead drop spot now. The signal site near the Palace Bridge had been blown to bits, as well its dead drop site, the telephone booth on the corner.

A message had come through a week before that the new signal site was at the Charité hospital, and the dead drop site at a bench in a small park across the street. Not the easiest place to get to. But she had finally decided to go make the mark and then the drop, requesting to meet there the following day. She clenched the chalk with one hand in her left pocket, and in her right, a crust of bread.

The following day Alice got there early. She had wedged the bread just beneath the bench footing at the far end, with the note of the time stuffed into the thickest part of the bread. It was gone, but she began to think of all the things that could have dislodged it—a city rat? There were plenty. A bird looking for crumbs? There was precious little to eat in the city. A park attendant picking up trash—would they really be that diligent to pick out a crust of bread? Or that hungry?

She sat with a schoolbook and pretended to study. But this was impossible. She had been waiting at least thirty minutes

267

when she saw a slender man approaching in what looked like work clothes. Dusty overalls and a workers' cap with fur-lined earflaps. There was something slightly familiar about the way he walked. He came up to the bench.

"Walter!"

"Ja."

"So you've known all along about us?"

"Ja."

"Does Papa know?"

"I don't think so."

"And you're not Rasa?"

"No. Not at all." He chuckled softly. "Not MI6 either."

"What are you?"

"SOE—Special Operations Executive."

"Oh yes, of course."

"So what's your problem?"

"I think it's a problem. Not sure."

"Just say it." He bent his head as he sat down and rested his elbows on his knees. She bent over as well. They appeared to be talking to the ground.

"Well, I think someone . . . uh . . . how should I put it . . . recognized . . ."

"Remembered your face?"

"Yes."

"Who?"

"A fellow in the Führerbunker." She paused. "A Were-wolf." She whispered the word. The word felt hot on her lips.

"Oh god!" Walter said softly. It was actually the softness of his reply that sent a chill through her.

"How many times has it happened?"

"Just once."

"Have you seen him again since then?"

"Yes, maybe twice."

"And no sign of recognition?"

"No, nothing." She swallowed. "Should I be extracted?"

"I'm not sure. I'll have to talk to my fios. I think they'll be reluctant. The quality of your information has been extremely good. Excellent. Particularly the continuing state of denial of Starling about the Allied situation. He refused to believe they've made such headway." Walter sighed.

"The Allies have just trapped another German division west of the Rhine River. And yet Starling still thinks he can win there, as you reported. It's going to be a complete debacle. The kind of information you're giving us is vital. Vital for the spirits of the Allied forces. Eisenhower himself is feasting on this intelligence. *Your* intelligence, Ute." He paused. "Starling is still planning this performance in the bunker—the *Götterdämmerung*?"

"Yes, the Werewolf are actually building scenery."

"If only they'd just stick to scenery and such nonsense." He paused again and inhaled before continuing. "Look, Ute, I must warn you about these Werewolf. They are really dangerous. They make the Gestapo look like clowns. They are trained killers. Their weapons are a slip-knotted garrote, a wire specially made for strangulation, or a Walther pistol with a silencer. You know about the mayor of Aachen?"

She shook her head.

"He was killed. Assassinated yesterday by a team of Werewolf." There was a long silence that seemed to engulf both of them. Walter extended his hand and patted her knee. "Believe me, Ute, I'll understand if you want to withdraw."

"No. The only place I want to withdraw to is . . ." Her words seemed to die on her lips as she thought of the golden cottage in the Cotswolds. But here she was, surrounded by darkness—the Starling, Fritz, and yes, even her own Louise! The thought startled her. "I have to go. Thank you, Walter." She got up and walked away.

THIRTY-THREE

TABLEAU MORTE

In the last week of March, the last kilometer of the Russian railway was laid across Poland to bring millions of tons of rockets, ammunition, fuel, and food to support the invasion of Berlin. The word of the railroad completion rattled the citizens of the city. They were racked with despair and anxiety, and completely exhausted. But in the Führerbunker, Hitler's favorite scene from the second opera, *The Ride of the Valkyries*, was being presented. The evening before, it had been the last act of *Götterdämmerung*. It seemed that the program was caught in an infinite cycle of Hitler's favorite scenes from all four operas.

For this scene of the ride, Alice stretched her mouth wide, as instructed, and the cry of the Valkyries ripped through the theater of the bunker. Not from Alice's throat, of course, but that of Martha Mödl, the famous soprano. Across the winged horse that Alice "rode," there was a dummy slung—a dead hero who she would transport to Valhalla. She peered out into the audience, where the Führer sat in the front row, transfixed. His pale gray eyes were riveted on the Valkyries, who rode their wooden horses to Valhalla.

Hours before, an urgent appeal had been broadcast on the radio—that every German should join the effort to kill. The words still rang in Alice's ears as she had prepared for the performance. "We must hit the enemy—every Bolshevik, every Englishman, every American—every traitor within our own city must be hit wherever we meet them. Our motto is conquer or die."

And then on the very next day, April 2, following the previous evening's performance, she was playing Brünnhilde again.

On April 9, dozens of well-known opponents of the regime were rounded up by the SS and Werewolf and sent to various concentration camps, where they were butchered.

On April 10, during a brief visit home, Alice and her parents were both eating dinner before she had to return to the Führerbunker when a radio announcer broke through. "Ladies and gentlemen, I would now like you to hear from a new broadcaster—a lovely lady. Yes indeed. We call her Lily the Werewolf."

A silky voice seeped into the kitchen as they sat around

the table eating yet another pea-meal and potato-skin concoction of Posie's.

"I am so savage," the voice began. "I am filled with rage. Lily the Werewolf is my name. I bite, I eat, I am not tame. My Werewolf teeth bite the enemy."

"Well, that certainly takes away one's appetite," Posie murmured. "Oh, what I wouldn't give for some beef tea and a smidge of Marmite on some bread—good bread, real bread."

On this same night two hours later, Alice was once again getting into her Valkyrie costume. The stage was set and painted with flames—the flames of the pyre upon which Brünnhilde would hurl herself in her last desperate act. Alice just had to get through this night. The snow had cleared. The bikes were waiting for them. Her father had managed to build three relatively sturdy bikes.

He had told Alice that the Russian troops were actually making 358 kilometers a day. Her family had to get out before they arrived. So far, the Russians had left absolute massacres in their wake. They wouldn't know that the Winfields were British citizens, spies, part of the Allied forces. They might not even care, Alan Winfield said.

Alice was backstage, waiting for the curtain to drop on the first scene, before the one she was to appear in. On the other side of the stage, she saw a girl named Ingrid, a kitchen worker, dressed in an outfit identical to her own— Brünnhilde. *How odd,* she thought.

Then, in that same moment, she gasped as she felt herself jerked backward. A knotted wire cut into her neck. She gasped for air. *I am being garroted.* The wire cut in deeper. The pain was excruciating, but the harder she resisted, the more it hurt. Her lungs felt as if they were on fire. Her head was being cut from her body. She saw her life guttering out of her like a candle flame with no air. There was no hope. Only a growing black void that filled her head. *I am dying.* Her thoughts came slowly. Her eyes slid upward . . . to be met by sky-blue Nazi eyes, white-blond hair across the brow.

Then suddenly the wire dropped. There was a split second of shock in the blue eyes, and then a thud on the floor. She looked down. The white-blond hair brushed his collar—and stuck in his neck was a hypodermic needle.

A hand grabbed hers. "Come along, dear."

"Louise!"

"Shush! Follow me."

Posie Winfield had been frying up some eggs, for which she had paid an astronomical price. She had just removed the pan from the burner as the two girls walked into the small basement apartment. She emitted a tiny shriek and dropped the pan. "Louise!!

"Yes, Mum."

"Alice—Alice What happened to your neck?"

"Uh . . . uh . . . it's hard to explain, Mum."

At that moment their father entered the tiny kitchen with a bicycle chain.

"What's . . . Louise?"

"Yes, Dad."

"Dad, we need another bike!" Alice said.

"Yes, yes. Give me fifteen minutes. I have all the parts."

During those fifteen minutes, Louise explained that she had acted as a double agent. "Same as you, Mum. But they wanted my face to be remembered."

"So you just pretended to be tired of your . . . your old face?"

"Not really. When I went to the director and said I might be considering surgery, he told me that there was a need for a young woman with a memorable face. They needed her to infiltrate this new paramilitary organization that was being created. The war was about to turn, he felt. With the Normandy invasion, and the Russians miraculously turning back the Germans. Plus, the Red Army was absolutely uncrushable. This new organization, the Werewolf, was started to terrorize Allied soldiers and any collaborators, spies and so on, as they pushed farther into Germany."

"And my cover was discovered? My face remembered?" Alice asked.

"I'm not sure. Your face wasn't exactly remembered, but word got out, maybe a month ago, that there was an infiltrator. Somehow a link was made to Stauffenberg. It was that link that finally convinced them that you were the infiltrator.

But look, Stauffenberg died almost nine months ago, and it's taken them all this time to get to you." Alan Winfield had reentered the room. "All right. Time to leave."

"Yes, right away. I can imagine that when they find Fritz, they will be here soon."

"They'll find him right away, won't they?"

"Not if Frau Weissmann has her way."

"Frau Weissmann!" Alice exclaimed.

"Yes, can't explain now. Later. Let me just say this. Frau Weissmann is not exactly a Frau."

"Wh . . . what is she?" Alice stammered.

"Colonel Reginald Griffith. A decathlon champion from the 1928 Olympics, I believe. Quite strong. She removed the body and took it to her quarters by a secret passage, and then fled the Führerbunker."

Alice blinked. "My head is spinning."

"Hey, at least it's still attached!" Louise said.

THIRTY-FOUR

TO THE ELBE

On the night of April 10, the four members of the Winfield family, with their bikes and backpacks, boarded the subway, or U-Bahn, train at Alexanderplatz, the number eight that headed west. They took it to the last station on the western line. The autobahn was clear of snow, but not of troops. Within ten kilometers they could see that they were closing in on the tail end of a German tank division.

Alan sighed. "Too bad we don't have tanks. The road ahead has already been bombed by the Allies. That's what you need—a tank—to get over it. We'll have to get off the Autobahn and go across these fields," Alan announced. "There will be country roads on the other side. Let's hope they weren't bombed."

"Mum," Alice said. "This looks so much like the field that we parachuted into."

"Well, the good news is that this would not be a good road for the army at all. But we're still heading west. And look, a sunny day, I think," Alan Winfield turned his head toward the east, where the dawn was just breaking.

Within five miles they came to a village. The sun was barely up, but there was an unusual bustle in the street as they rode through.

An elderly man on a cane walked up to Alice. He looked delighted as he greeted the four Winfields.

"Willkommen in unserem Dorf. Es wird bald amerikanisch sein."

"What?" Posie exclaimed.

"Ah yes, Frau. The Americans have reached Magdeburg, and tomorrow they will cross the Elbe. We are celebrating!" He giggled. Then, in a very somber voice, "So much better to be captured by the Americans than the Russians."

They all suddenly realized that they could hear the crackle of radios pouring out from open windows in the village.

"It's Alvar!" Alice gasped. Alvar Lidell was their favorite newsreader from the BBC. The four Winfields rushed to the window from which the familiar voice was coming.

"The American Ninth Army today reached the city of Magdeburg. They are expected to establish a link between their troops and the Russians on the east bank of the Elbe. This should occur in a matter of days . . ." Alvar Lidell's crisp voice seeped into the air. Posie closed her eyes, as if she was tasting the most delicious thing in the world.

"Mum, you look so happy. Like when you smell good things cooking."

"I am savoring his voice. It's so, so wonderful. It's Sunday roast and pudding. It's fish-and-chips." She sighed. "Indulge me children. May I quote Mr. Browning?

"Oh, to be in England
Now that April's there
And whoever wakes in England
Sees, some morning, unaware,
That the lowest boughs and the brushwood sheaf
Round the elm-tree bole are in tiny leaf,
While the chaffinch sings on the orchard bough
In England—now!"

As she recited the Robert Browning poem, Alice thought of their cottage in the Cotswolds with its trailing ribbons of roses and ivy. The cottage softly glowing softly like a beacon of peace and comfort and happiness.

Alan Winfield came up and gave his wife a hug and an extra squeeze around her shoulders. "Come along, old gal. We've got to push on!" He pressed his lips together, which he often did when he was in deep thought.

"What is it, Dad?"

"I'm calculating. If the Americans just arrived at Magdeburg, and Alvar said something about the Red Army closing in on Torgau, there are maybe two hundred kilometers between them." He pulled a compass out from his pants pocket. "We are closer to the Russians than the Americans. We don't want that!" he said forcefully. "We have to press on. We have to get to the Elbe before the Red Army does."

No one asked why. They knew why. The Red Army was brutal, particularly to women. The soldiers didn't care if they were German, American, or British. They were savages.

The people in the village were actually quite helpful. The Winfields' cover story was that they desperately need to get to the next village, where their eldest daughter was expecting a baby. And when they got to Beendorf, they told the same story and moved on to the next village.

And so they went. Rarely stopping to rest, they pushed through a rainstorm and a flurry of snow showers. When they did rest, they sought culverts and wooded areas. They had made good time considering they were walking their bikes for miles on end. The bikes themselves had suffered flat tires and other problems. But Alan had brought a small pump with him, glue, and patching material. In the villages, people were very supportive of the raggedy family trying to get to their eldest daughter and what would be their first grandchild. The people shared what they had, which wasn't much.

Well past midnight on this particular evening, they had retreated to a thickly wooded patch half a kilometer from the road. They could hear the gunfire and the rumble of tanks—the Red Army tanks, Alan said. "It seems we and the Russians are proceeding together. The Russians undoubtedly are trying to get the German Twelfth Army, which is stationed at Dessau and most likely preparing for the Americans' Ninth Army. I'd estimate that we're twenty miles from the Elbe River." He sighed. And stared down at the pieces of thick felt in his hands. "We could tear up a coat and improvise, with these brake pads gone. But I doubt I can repair them. And honestly it's too dangerous right now to proceed on the open road." He looked up at his family. "We're simply going to have to walk . . . walk right into the Americans' arms. No other way."

They would rest briefly. Alice volunteered to stand watch at the base of a spruce tree, where she propped herself again its trunk and watched the gray of the night dissolve. Within moments, the rest of the Winfields were slipping into a thin sleep. No one slept deeply anymore. The sky began to swell with clouds as the dawn broke, ugly and red. It seemed to Alice as if the war had literally bled into the sky, as if the earth had hemorrhaged with its burden of the dead and the dying and simply could absorb no more. No birds spilled their song into the dawn sky. There was only the distant pounding of artillery.

The morning was cold, and they were wrapped up in every scrap of clothing they had. A shallow layer of ground fog was beginning to rise as Alice unwrapped a candy bar. She was just about to bite into it when a small figure emerged from a thicket of slender birches not twenty feet away.

My god! she thought. It was a child dressed in a raggedy coat that was several sizes too big. A flat hat, also too large, with a shiny black visor that almost covered his eyes. He carried a huge, ancient-looking weapon. And on his sleeve he wore an armband—a Volkssturm armband. Alice heard her father say, "Good lord, I haven't seen one of those bolt action rifles since the Great War and Verdun."

"Ja, ja. As good as a Panzerfaust—a tank fist. I can blow up a tank with this." A high, piping voice emanated from somewhere under the dark visor.

"I'm sure you can, young man."

The boy, who could not have been more than eight or nine years old, smiled slightly and narrowed his eyes.

"I'm going to kill you. Kill you all. I'm from the people's army."

"Uh . . . before you kill us, might you tell us your name?" Alice asked.

"Why?" the child snarled.

"I . . . I just feel that it's polite."

"But you'll be dead. Why do you need to know? You going to tattle on me to God? God is on my side."

"And do you know what side we are on?" Alan asked. By this point, Posie and Louise were wide awake.

"Yes, yes, it would be proper, dear, for us to introduce ourselves," Posie spoke in her most motherly voice.

"My name is Max!" the boy blurted out.

"Max!" Alice exclaimed. "Like Max and Moritz."

"Yes," the boy cried with sheer delight. "You like Max and Moritz?"

"My very favorite comic strip in the whole wide world. I'm going to be a teacher when I grow up. And I'm going to insist

282

that for homework every night, every kid has to read a Max and Moritz cartoon. And then we're going to learn how to draw the characters." The boy's eyes grew wide.

"What's your favorite Max and Moritz story?" he asked.

Alice put one finger thoughtfully against her cheek as if thinking. "Well it's a tie, really. I love the one where they put the beetles in the uncle's bed, but I also like the one about the Widow Bolte and the frying chickens."

"Oh, that one is so funny! And the part where they get the fishing rods and climb onto the roof of the barn and then fish for the frying chickens and then the widow . . ." He now sounded like every eight-year-old boy Alice had ever encountered. They had to tell you every single part of a complicated plot in any story—a movie, a book, or a comic strip. "You know what?" Max's brown eyes opened even wider as he looked at Posie Winfield, whose own eyes were fixed on the huge rifle. "Your mum over there looks a lot like the Widow Bolte."

"Hmmm . . ." Alice said in a reflective tone. "I don't quite see it. But maybe."

"Maybe not!" flashed Posie. "I'm not nearly as fat as the Widow Bolte."

"Oh, you read comic strips too!" Max was clearly delighted.

"Not that much, but I've seen the ones my daughter reads."

"Well, you're not as fat, but there's something about your face."

Posie smiled. Alice thought she saw the shimmer of tears welling up in her mother's eyes.

"Max," said Alice. "Come over here and sit beside me and tell me the rest. Want some chocolate? I have a Good Chew here. I can share it with you."

"You have a Good Chew?"

"Indeed I do." Without a thought, the boy laid down his gun and came and sat by Alice.

For the next twenty minutes, they talked Max and Moritz stories and ate candy, for the Winfields had packed at least two dozen bars. When Alice began to tell the one about Max and the angry teacher, Max burst out. "Oh, I didn't know that one! The teacher stories are my sister's favorite!"

"Ah, then you can tell her this one."

His face suddenly turned somber.

"Nope," he said crisply. "She's dead."

"I'm so sorry to hear that." Alice said.

"My mum and dad too."

"Oh dear," Posie moaned softly. She stood up and walked over to where he sat next to Alice. "Tell me, Max, would you like to join us?"

He didn't answer for what seemed to Alice as the longest time. He looked over at the gun he had laid on the ground. There was an unbearable tension that seemed to seize the air.

"Are you going to surrender?" he asked.

"You can call it what you like, son." Alan Winfield walked up to him. "But we are going to live, and you still have a lot of growing to do."

"Yes, sir. My father was six feet three inches tall."

"Oh, I bet you'll be too," Alan Winfield said. "Come along, son." Alice watched her father put a hand on the boy's shoulder. Then Max reached up and took Alan's hand, and they all began to walk west.

They left their bikes in the woods and walked several miles until they reached the Elbe River. They spent hours crouched behind the wreckage of a panzer tank on the east side of the Elbe and watched. The bridge that spanned the river had been destroyed, and what was left was a twisted mass of steel rearing from the water like a warped sea monster.

"How will we get across?" Louise whispered. "The war is over, but we're stuck here."

"Look!" Alan Winfield said. "Look at those soldiers!"

Two soldiers were scrambling over the crumpled remains of the bridge. One carried a Russian flag, the other an American flag.

"They're climbing out on that broken bridge," Alice whispered. "I can't believe it."

"They're shaking hands," Louise said.

"We're going home!" Posie sighed as tears streamed down her face. She turned toward Max. "Would you like to come all the way home with us, Max?"

"Where is home?" His little face looked up at her.

"England, child. England!"

EPILOGUE

Five days later on a transport ship across the English Channel, Alice and Louise stood by the railing, watching the coast of England emerge. The public address system crackled to life. Not with the voice of the captain, but of BBC newscaster Alvar Lidell.

"This is London Calling. Here is a dispatch just in. German radio minutes ago announced that Hitler is dead. I'll repeat that. Hitler is dead. He died of a self-inflicted gunshot wound, forty hours after marrying Eva Braun. Some say that an aria from his favorite composer, Richard Wagner, was playing at the time of his suicide."

Louise turned to Alice. "My little Valkyrie. Mission accomplished!"

"No Valhalla for him!" Alice muttered. She sighed. "I've

been to hell and back." Then she sighed again. "I'm retiring."

"At the ripe old age of fourteen, you're retiring?"

"Almost fifteen," Alice replied. "remember—or maybe you don't—you missed my fourteenth.

"And your face?"

"I like my face—just the way it is." She paused. Then, in barely a whisper, she said to herself, "Yes. Just the way it is."

I have had an endless fascination with World War Two. So *Faceless* is my fourth book about this war. I would first like to give thanks to those who are not here—the Greatest Generation. From that generation I need to single out a few: my uncle Jack Hurwitz, who was in the Battle of the Bulge and served as a radio operator; my aunt Mildred Falender Hurwitz, who enlisted as a WAVE, a branch of the United States Naval Reserve unit; and my cousin Jack Lasky, who served in North Africa under the command of General George S. Patton.

I would also like to acknowledge the lives of more than a dozen distant cousins who died in the Nazi concentration camps.

These people are all gone, but thank you, Uncle Jack and Cousin Jack and Aunt Mildi, for your service. And to my cousins who died, a blessing on your memory.

But there are those who are living who helped me so much with this book. First, my editor Alyson Day at Harper Collins: thanks for her expert eye and delicate touch with a manuscript. Also, eternal gratitude to Tom Ricks, who knows wars and warfare and has deep insights into military history. Tom graciously allowed me to poke around in his cellar library and sift through his enormous collection of books on World War II, secret intelligence agencies, and spycraft.

A deep thanks to my son-in-law, Andrew Nelles, who has

seen war up close as a photo journalist and has twice gone to Afghanistan to document that war. Andrew's deep knowledge of aircraft and weaponry, both past and present, was very important for this book. Whom else could I have asked about the minutia of details concerning the Lysander aircraft that dropped Alice and her mom, Posie, into Germany?

And finally, I am eternally grateful to my husband, Christopher Knight, who has for more than fifty years encouraged and cheered me on. No one matches Chris for patience with a wife who is a total Luddite when it comes to electronics and basically other technology ranging from toasters (yes, I consider a toaster not high-tech but still a problem for me) to computers.

AUTHOR'S NOTE

The novel *Faceless* is the fourth book I have written about World War Two—a war that started six years before I was born and ended two months before my first birthday. What did I know about this war at a very young age, growing up in Indiana, so far from those battlegrounds?

I knew that my uncle Jacob Hurwitz was a radio operator during the Battle of the Bulge, scrambling around in the Ardennes with a transmitter radio strapped to his back, dodging land mines and Nazis. This was Hitler's last gasp. Nineteen thousand American troops killed in action, 47,500 wounded. I knew that my Aunt Mildred Falender Hurwitz was a lieutenant in the WAVES, the women's branch of the United States Naval Reserve, and that she was married to Jacob in her snappy WAVES uniform. And that she sometimes wore it after the war for Thanksgiving dinners.

I knew that my cousin Jack Lasky, twenty years older than me, was one of the 33,000 men who served under General George Patton in the North African Campaign.

That's what I knew.

This is a war that has endlessly fascinated me. When I was in the fifth grade, I started reading books about the war, both fiction and nonfiction. Yes, I did read a lot about the Holocaust. But I actually read more about the war itself. I read *Stalag 17* and *Slaughterhouse Five*. I had to read *Slaughterhouse Five* because it was by Kurt Vonnegut, who came from my hometown! I read *From Here to Eternity*. I read *The Naked and the*

Dead when I was in the sixth grade. Why did I read it? Because my parents were reading it. I read *The Young Lions* by Irwin Shaw and *A Bell for Adano* by John Hersey. And of course I read *The Diary of a Young Girl* by Anne Frank, and in the seventh grade I read Elie Wiesel's book *Night*.

I liked battle books more, and I was simply crazy for Winston Churchill. I read everything I could about him. But I did not read *The Gathering Storm*, which both my parents read and of which we had two copies. My mom moved one to my bedroom, knowing how much I loved Churchill. I tried. I was in the sixth grade then, but I couldn't get past the first ten pages. However, *The Bridge Over the River Kwai* had been translated from French into English when I was ten years old, and I read that and then saw the movie three times.

I was steeped in these war stories since I was a middle grader. It came as no surprise to me that when I grew up and became a writer, I would eventually write a war book. Now I've written four. The first book was *Ashes*, set in Berlin in 1933. It centered around the Nazi book burnings in May of that year. The second book, *The Extra*, was the story of a Roma who was plucked from a Roma internment camp and forced to work in a movie being made by Hitler's favorite filmmaker, Leni Riefenstahl. The third was *Night Witches*, the story of the heroic young Russian women who flew intrepid bombing missions in the defense of Stalingrad and then chased the Nazis all the way back to Germany.

What is interesting is that I have never told any of these war stories from a Jewish point of view, yet eighteen cousins of my generation perished in extermination camps. Why would I not tell a story from the Jewish point of view? The answer is simple. I always wanted to explore what non-Jewish people were thinking. Were they merely complicit? Or was there something deeper? What was going through their minds? Did they have any empathy, like Oskar Schindler, in some way?

In my own World War Two novels I wanted to get beyond the tropes, the predictable narratives, and find the one narrative of empathy—empathy from the least expected sources. For me it is this search for empathy that is inspiring and can be extraordinary.

There is a question that I often have to field: "You're Jewish, so why don't you have more Jewish content in your war books?" The answer is that I want to explore more than just writing about my Judaism. And I have written about my Judaism in many books—*The Night Journey, Broken Song, Marven of the Great North Woods, Blood Secret.* I'll continue to do so.

But it is when I am not in my own skin but writing through the eyes of another that I am at my most revolutionary, my most authentic, and able to upend traditional perspectives.

I know that I can tell a more compassionate war story if I step into another person's skin and begin to search for the humanity, the empathy that I continue to believe lurks in every human's soul.

HISTORICAL FIGURES FEATURED—BACKGROUND INFORMATION

While many of the characters in this book are made up, some are real people. Here is background information on some of the historical figures that Alice encounters.

Adolf Hitler was an Austrian-born German politician who was dictator of Germany from 1933 to 1945. He rose to power as the leader of the Nazi Party, becoming chancellor in 1933 and then Führer in 1934. During his dictatorship, he initiated World War II and the Holocaust, the genocide of six million European Jews during the war.

Eva Braun was the companion of Adolf Hitler for several years. She met Hitler in Munich when she was seventeen years old. For less than forty hours, she was his wife. They committed suicide together on April 30, 1945.

Joseph Goebbels was minister of propaganda for Nazi Germany from 1933 to 1945. He and his wife, Magda, committed suicide on May 1, 1945.

Hermann Göring is known for being one of the primary architects of the Third Reich Nazi police state in Germany. He established the Gestapo secret police and concentration camps. In addition, he organized the plundering of art collected by prominent Jewish families—the Rothschilds, the Wildensteins, and the Rosenbergs. He was arrested and found guilty in the subsequent Nuremberg war trials and sentenced to death. He committed suicide shortly before his execution.

Emmy Göring was the wife of Hermann.

Claus von Stauffenberg was a German army officer best known for Operation Valkyrie, his failed attempt, on July 20, 1944, to assassinate Adolf Hitler at the Wolf's Lair. He was arrested a short time after this. He received a death sentence and was shot at midnight by a firing squad in the courtyard of the Bendlerblock in Berlin.

Winifred Wagner, born in England, was the daughter-in-law of Richard Wagner, the composer of many operas, including the Ring Cycle. She had married Wagner's son, Siegfried, who was the director of the Bayreuth Festival. After his death she became the director of the festival. She was passionately devoted to Hitler and the Nazi regime. She died in 1980.

Martin Bormann was head of the German Nazi Party Chancellery and Adolf Hitler's private secretary. He became party minister of the National Socialist German Workers' party after Hitler's suicide on April 30, 1945, and later fled and is thought to have committed suicide in May 1945.

Elisabeth Kalhammer was Hitler's housekeeper at the Berghof. She began when she was nineteen years old. She kept her job a secret for seventy years following Hitler's death.

Traudl Junge was Hitler's last personal secretary. Hitler called upon her to type out his will shortly before he committed suicide.

INSPIRATION FOR FACELESS CONDITION

Several years ago, I read a novel about a boy who had witnessed a murder but could not remember the murderer's face. It turned out that he had a cognitive disorder called prosopagnosia, in which people simply cannot register other people's faces. It wasn't the face itself that triggered this response. It was something in that person's brain. A kind of dyslexia that made them unable to recall faces. So, I started thinking, what if it were the reverse? What if there was a small group of people whose faces in and of themselves were simply not memorable. What if the entire world had this cognitive disorder for those particular people? Wouldn't a person with such a face make a great spy? Hence the Rasas, as in Tabula Rasa, came to be.